MIGHTY

AN ANTHOLOGY OF DISABLED SUPERHEROES

EDITED BY EMILY GILLESPIE AND JENNIFER LEE ROSSMAN

Renaissance.
Diverse Canadian Voices

pressesrenaissancepress.ca

MIGHTY ©2023 edited by Emily Gillespie and Jennifer Lee Rossman. PUTTING A BEE IN THEIR BONNET © Cait Gordon. JOY JUMPERS © *Joy Jumpers* by KS Palakovic DEATH IN THE RAIN © Dave Lerner. GRANNY SMITH © Polly Orr. THE GLAUC BITCHES © Melissa Yi MIND BENDER by Rowan Marci. MUTANT PRIDE © Shannon Barnsley. INVISIBLE DEE © E.D.E. Bell. HOLD STEADY AGAINST THE TIDE © Beatrice Morgan. HELL WEEK © Emma Hardy. CAPTAIN MAVEN AND THE ICE QUEEN © Jamieson Wolf. INSTITUTING A CYCLE OF VIOLENCE © Matthew Del Papa. THINKING *INSIDE* THE BOX © Holly Schofield. MASKING UP © Erin Rockfort.

First edition 2023

Cover art and design by Nathan Frechette. Interior design by Diana Galván Mejía. Copy editing by Aliya Bartmon.

Legal deposit, Library and Archives Canada, October 2023.

Paperback ISBN: 978-1-990086-53
Ebook ISBN: 978-1-990086-64

Renaissance Press | pressesrenaissancepress.ca

Renaissance acknowledges that it is hosted on the traditional, unceded land of the Anishinabek, the Kanien'kehá'ka, and the Omàmìwininìwag. We acknowledge the privileges and comforts that colonialism has granted us and vow to use this privilege to disrupt colonialism by lifting up the voices of marginalized humans who continue to suffer its ongoing repercussions.

Printed in Gatineau

We gratefully acknowledge the support of the Canada Council for the Arts.

Conseil des Arts du Canada　　**Canada Council for the Arts**

To my late Dad,
Jack Gillespie, my first hero.
— Emily Gillespie

For all my future heroes,
especially those who can't see their capes yet
— Jennifer Lee Rossman

TABLE OF CONTENTS

FROM THE EDITORS

As origin stories go, "It was a joke" doesn't have quite the same impact as getting bitten by a radioactive spider or being the only survivor of a dying planet—but sometimes the best stories are a little silly.

Mighty did, indeed, start with a joke. Specifically, that "differently abled"—a euphemism for "disabled" that many disabled people consider ableist—is "a politically correct term for X-Men."

That joke mutated into an idea about something bigger, a way to bring disabled voices together to make a difference. Soon I had our amazing publisher Nathan approaching me and asking if I wanted to put a team together.

—Jennifer

I am proud of this collection of 14 own-voices stories that engage with adventure, heroism, and the reality of living our best disabled lives. As a multiply disabled person, I don't often see myself represented as a hero, unless it slips into the cringy space of the super-Crip, or disability inspiration porn.

Thanks to the authors, the heroes in these stories, and Nathan and Jennifer for including me in this project. May it help redefine how we think about disability and heroes.

—Emily

In the 14 stories we've assembled here, our authors take on the superhero genre like only disabled people can, playing with and subverting the sometimes harmful tropes to make saving the world (or just one small part of it) accessible and inclusive for everyone.

It is our honor to share them with you and we hope you enjoy them as much as we do.

—Jennifer and Emily

FOREWORD
WE CAN BE HEROES?
SUPER!

BY CAIT GORDON

I had the pleasure as co-editor of the award-nominated anthology, *Nothing Without Us*, of being introduced to the incredible writing talent of Jennifer Lee Rossman and Emily Gillespie. Their stories— "Names" and "No Room at the Inn," respectively—grabbed Talia C. Johnson and me immediately as must-haves for that collection. At the time, the catchphrase for that anthology was, "We are the heroes, not the sidekicks." And now, Jennifer and Emily have gone even further as co-editors to cast disabled folks not only as heroes, but as superheroes! Mighty ones at that!

Those of us who are disabled, d/Deaf, Blind, neurodivergent, and/or who manage mental illness and/or chronic conditions don't find it farfetched to imagine ourselves as superheroes. We defy a lot of villainy in our everyday lives—oftentimes, in the form of ableism and lack of accessibility—and my least favourite: inspiration porn.

That last trope refers to narratives about "overcoming disability" in a way that is supposed to inspire everyone to be the same. There's a real stigma against us choosing to accept and work with our disabilities, which often leads to many of us having to overcome internalized ableism in order to thrive.

In *Mighty: An Anthology of Superheroes*, our protagonists defy the odds within oppressive realities while still managing the traits of their disability, and the traits or symptoms of these lead characters can be more than just a slight distraction. I'll even go so far as saying that loudness itself represents a sort of "kryptonite" for Reactor Woman in Dave Lerner's "Death in the Rain." Being someone who deals with auditory sensory issues, I could absolutely relate to how that could be a major obstacle, even for a superhero. However, it's nice to know that having a support faerie/spirit is an option to help with anxiety, like how Sprightly assists our superhero in "Granny Smith" by Polly Orr. It's comforting as well to realize one can continue to save the day well into one's 70s and that comfy knit costumes with infinity pockets are a thing. Melissa Yi taught me a valuable lesson: one should never mess with "The Glauc Bitches." They not only save mistreated animals from gross humans, but these women also have various powers based on the progress of their glaucoma—which causes these powers to increase, not diminish. Another disability representation that really wowed me for a superhero to have to push through while heroing was premenstrual dysphoric disorder (PMDD). I want to congratulate the editors of this anthology for including "Hell Week" by Emma Hardy. In real life, very few folks seem to want to discuss this type of disability/chronic condition, and I was rooting the entire time for Terra confronting her multiverse selves.

Language matters. How we identify matters. I remember being on a panel when Jennifer Lee Rossman joked that the expression differently abled was a politically correct term for X-men. (I still love this so hard.) So, of course, I was delighted to see the word "mutant" in Shannon Barnsley's "Mutant Pride" regarded with the same esteem as many of us use the word "disabled." As in: "Just say mutant, folks. Mutant is not a bad word." And no, I will not Google the term "enhanced individual." Thanks for the tip.

But sometimes, to quote Ted Lasso, we lead characters are a "work in prog-mess." That's what I found so honest about Jada in Rowan Marci's "Mind Bender." Sometimes we might be finding our way between hero and villain, not wanting to be the latter, but not exactly sure how to be the former. Sometimes we need to acknowledge that we've got some learning to do. I adore nuance and feel it's so important to have those grey areas—the characters who are still on the path to discovering the heroes within themselves.

And further into the realm of honesty, lateral ableism—which is the ableism found within disability communities themselves—is a harsh reality. So, when I caught those moments in E.D.E. Bell's "Invisible Dee," I nearly nodded until my head fell off. Disabilities that aren't outwardly spotted, known as invisible disabilities, are often disregarded, discounted, causing folks to be pushed to the margins. When this happens, they frequently ask themselves, "Am I disabled enough to be included?" Yes. Yes, you are. Also, and someone act on this right away—somebody please give Dee some food that fits her dietary requirements! She needs to eat!

What is so important about creating stories based on our lived experiences is that we can craft the heroes we want to be while not hiding who we actually are. We don't need "cures" in order to be heroic. We can have powers without remedies—all we need is a sense of justice and a whole lotta guts. The beauty of an anthology like *Mighty* is that one can feel the authenticity of the storytelling: the humour, the guilt, the anger, the loss, and the triumph. What's great about having a collection curated by editors who are also disabled and neurodivergent is that we disabled creatives can submit our work with the confidence it can be recognized and understood. And if the work is not accepted, we can feel pretty sure it wasn't dismissed with that infamous phrase, "I couldn't relate to the characters."

In closing, I invite you to dive into this anthology because every story in it has depth and meaning. Share it far and wide! Encourage folks to ask for it in their local bookstores and libraries. But also, I offer a challenge to you—who are disabled, d/Deaf, Blind, neurofabulous, and/or those of you who manage chronic conditions and/or mental illnesses:

Be mighty. Write your heroes. Publish your zines. Make audio books. Do spoken word or perform a poetry slam using sign language. Create anthologies of your own. We need more works out there that are by us and for us. Defy the character depictions that people who don't share our lived experiences have written of us. Rewrite those tropes. Turn harmful narratives upside down or yeet them into the sun. Take centre stage with heroes that blow us all away with their awesome.

Because, and apologies to the late, great David Bowie:
We can be heroes…for more than one day.

— Cait Gordon, author of Iris and the Crew Tear Through Space *and co-editor of* Nothing Without Us *and* Nothing Without Us Too

PUTTING A BEE IN THEIR BONNET

BY CAIT GORDON

CN: Ableism, Applied Behavioural Analysis (ABA), lightning strike causing injury

Under a gloomy sky filled with cotton candy clouds that look like they've been dipped in soot, I stand at the bus stop outside the learning centre downtown, shoving ear-pods in my skull holes. I'm still angry I forgot to bring headphones that block out more sound. Wish I could block out the entire morning, to be honest.

At least now I have my favourite Scandinavian foursome to lull my aural—as in audio—sense. Truly, I have no idea how often I've listened to "Dancing Queen." Maybe a bazillion times. But to me, it's always one playback too few of the required dosage.

Streaming the bouncy disco beat into my brain, I find myself longing to have the time of my life. But I keep getting flashbacks from that woman in the writing class I teach; the memory of her nonsense this morning interrupts my much-needed harmonies.

"But you're a *perrrson!*" (It sure felt like Susan had extended that first syllable.)

"Yes, I am a person. Thank you for recognizing this. And as I explained, I'm more comfortable calling myself autistic. In fact, many of us prefer identity-first language and—"

"Well!" she'd blurted with a Karen-like *harumph*. "My *nephew* has autism, and my *sister* is an Autism Mom Warrior, so she told me…"

I know at this moment I'd projected The Stare™. (It makes me happy to picture that little trademark symbol in my head, as if I'm using The Stare with permission from a neurodivergent person who had created it just for us.) Sometimes my prolonged gaze prompts people to shut up, but I'm guessing Susan was immune to it.

Why is it that people who don't share certain lived experiences can be so insistent on speaking over those who have? Is this a trait of the "normals?" Should we host an annual fundraiser?

Yes, People with Neurotypicalism are persons too! We can teach them how to reduce their need for small talk, putting all their hopes into yoga, and violently debating skinny jeans! Stay positive! You can fit into our puzzle if you try really hard! One day, we will find a cure!

Yeah, I'm being snarky. Some of my Autie buds say snark is a superpower, but even though I know they're being jokey, I kind of hate how Autistics are said to have superpowers—that just isn't a thing.

"Take a Chance on Me" is next on my playlist. It's not my favourite, but it always makes me chuckle because of the repetition of the lyrics as background vocals. Sometimes when I need to self-regulate, I sing that part to myself. No matter where I am, too. I've stopped caring what people think of me. It's nice being in my 50s.

Rumble-rumble goes the sky. A storm is imminent. And the bus is late… again.

I open up a social media app and as usual, see the posts of friends who are fed up with all the ABA garbage that's trending these days. I mean Applied Behaviour Analysis, of course—what a lot of us call conversion therapy to make children "less autistic." Wonderfully dehumanizing, in my opinion. Imagine thinking we don't even start out as real people, like we're some meat chassis that must be programmed by neurotypicals (NTs for short).

Sheesh. At least Susan says I'm a *perrrson*. Mind you, I half wonder if that's the only way people like her would recognize our personhood, through eradicating our autistic identity.

More rumblies. I'm not afraid of storms, but my mother's fretting comes into my head: *"Don't use anything electronic during a thunderstorm. You'll get electrocuted—or worse!"* Not sure what could be worse than getting electrocuted. Except maybe having to listen to Susan and all the paaarents who discuss Everything They Know About Autism. That, along with scratchy clothes and gluey food would be my Hell.

Holy cheese, where is the flipping bus? Also, where is everyone? This stop is typically packed.

More thunder makes me jolt. Figuratively, that is. I feel my anxiety heighten because this is weird.

"Take-a-chance," I mutter on repeat as a type of soothing mantra. It's funny how churning the words this way reminds me of an old-timey train. Gosh, I love trains. Autistic Trope Unlocked, I know. But trains are awesome. And I can pee anytime I want!

My legs are getting achy from standing, so I lean against the metallic pole of the bus stop sign. They recently changed the location of the stop from down the street, so it's one of those temporary setups until they move the bus shelter. Bracing myself for an annoyingly long wait, I blare the music through my pods while continuing my disco-train chant.

"Hey!" shouts a passerby who is jogging to safety. "There's a lightning warning for this area! Go inside the store behind you, quick!"

I can't fully focus on their words because I'm responding to a thread where someone is arguing to promote "Gentle ABA."

"There's no such thing," I type on my app. "That's like saying you're going to wallop my brain with a gentle mallet!" Still leaning against the metal pole, I press the Reply button and...

ZOLT!!!

■ .■ ■ ■ ■ ■.-■ ■ --- ■ ■ ■ ■

"Cayleen? Cayleen... can you hear my voice?"

I can, but it sounds like someone is speaking in slow motion. Reminds me of when I was a kid, and I held the record back on the turntable to reduce the speed and make the voices go deeper. Amused me to no end.

Whoever's speaking now is also shaking me. Guess that makes sense because if I couldn't hear, I'd not reply at all. Points for accommodation? My head feels strange. Maybe because this bed feels like concrete.

More shaking and more words are happening, "Cayleen? Do you know where you are?"

"Sol III?" Yeah, that's not my joke. That's my BFF's go-to answer. I guess it is kinda funny.

"Okay, she's responsive." The voice sounds more like a tenor than a bass now. Maybe my brain stopped slowing down the record on the turntable.

"Cayleen, can you open your eyes?" asks another voice that sounds more femme.

I try to, but there's a light shining, so I cringe and shut my lids fast.

"Can ya just not?" I say. "Sensory stuff!"

"What do you mean?" the voice with a higher pitch says.

"I'm autistic. Lights and sounds can sometimes trigger me into overload."

"Oh." The predictable pregnant pause is next. "Um, is there anyone else we can phone to answer our questions about you?"

I open my eyes in reflex. At least the light is turned off. "I'm sorry?"

A blond woman with a spray-tan, swooshy ponytail, and an EMT uniform is the higher voice. She's also looking at me kinda oddly. That thing where someone is smiling with their mouth, but their eyes seem wary.

"Good!" she says. "Very good! You can make eye contact. Very well done!"

Is she okay? I almost ask her this.

"Now, I'm going to speak *really clearly*, so you can understand me, okay?"

I blink.

"You were… struck by lightning… do you know what that means?"

I can't tell if I'm supposed to be angry here or accept that this is just how she communicates. But I nod.

PUTTING A BEE IN THEIR BONNET

"Your vitals… are stable. Heart rate is great! You're… so… lucky. But we'd like… to… have you assessed further. Would that… be… all right?"

She's nodding as she speaks with a tone I've often heard NT folks use with toddlers. Decision made—I'm choosing to be pissed off.

"Yeah, that's fine," I growl with a scowl. No time to enjoy how those words rhyme.

The other EMT, the brunette tenor with ivory skin and a sunburnt nose, is holding my medical info card from my wallet. He taps the shoulder of his colleague and says, "Bev, I think she's high-functioning."

"Oh, I'm sorry," Bev the Ponytail says to me. "I didn't realize you're high functioning. You must only have mild autism."

That does it. I can feel the meltdown imminent, as if steam will shoot out of my ears. I glare at them both, The Stare™ armed and ready, and feel something, hard to describe what—an energy of sorts—push out of me.

What the heckin' heck?

Next thing I know, Tenor EMT and Ponytail EMT begin shaking their shoulders to a beat they somehow both hear, and the *next* next thing I know, they're singing the chorus to "S.O.S." Like, the song by ABBA. They're dancing too, right there, right on the sidewalk. Ah, sidewalk! That's why this "bed" was so hard.

But this is concerning. Am I hallucinating? Did I hit my head that hard? I slowly sit up and scan my surroundings. Several teens are laughing at the paramedics while videoing them on their cellphones.

"I didn't know you guys were allowed to do flash-mob type stuff!" cried one of them, scanning the area. "Where are all the others?"

Distracted by the weirdness of it all, I calm down, and the EMTs stop their performance. The disappointed teens go, "Awww."

Yeah, maybe I should get out of here. Don't think I'll receive the medical care I need. Not from these two.

Bolting from awkward situations is something I can manage. In fact, I've been honing that skill since childhood. Despite my headache, I run like I'm training for a medal.

■ ■■ ■ ■■■ ■ ■ ■ ■■ ■■■

Thankfully, I'm on another bus. Head is still a bit spinny, but this route will take me to the health complex near home. They have all kinds of clinics there, so someone should be able to tell me something. My therapist is also at that location, so I know the place well.

Across from me, a silver-haired man with a youngish face is absorbed in the contents of his laptop screen while a little girl in a purple dress with white polka-dots points to the book on her own lap and tries to explain to him all about dinosaurs. I love dinosaurs and enjoyed spouting their names out of the book I carried everywhere when I was four. *Diplodocus* and *Triceratops* are still my faves. I'm reminded of a British soap that always had this woman with three curlers on the front of her hairline. I always called her *Triceratops*.

The girl is quite animated as she speaks, flapping her hands with joy as her raven-haired ringlets also appear to bounce with delight. Her energy is infectious, and I find myself smiling and tapping my fingertips in solidarity. Chronic pain makes it hard for me to flap, so I tap.

Papa is not having it, though. "Shawna! Quiet hands! Now!" He takes away her picture book with the *T. rex* on the cover and slams it on the empty seat beside him. *His* hands don't seem that quiet to me.

"Sorry, Daddy."

I watch her face intently as the tears well. Something also wells in me, but it isn't tears. I feel it in my core, under my diaphragm, then into my sternum. Another force to accompany The Stare™ shooting from my eyes. The energy is unstoppable, but I find myself unwilling to halt it and instead direct it right at the target of my choosing.

Next thing I know, an arpeggiated guitar emits from the man's laptop. Instead of wondering why the instrumental began, he looks up from his work and down at his tear-filled child, then gently wipes her cheek while singing "Slipping Through My Fingers." I have to admit, his voice has an exquisite male-alto tone.

The words come forth about capturing every minute and admitting that he can't see what's in her mind. She smiles at this unique attention she's being paid and waves her hands to the rhythm of his voice, imitating his own hand movements, until she receives her book back. When he's done with the song, I let go of whatever in me is causing this to happen.

There's not a dry eye on the bus. Except mine. My eyes are a desert.

I try to remain calm for the rest of the ride, hoping that this kid will have a parent who remembers to love her as she is and not force her to be something she isn't. At least Papa is cuddling her, the laptop forgotten for the time being.

Ding! It's my stop. I need to transfer buses. Gosh, my head hurts.

I stumble outside and manage to weave over to the stop in front of the university. I'm shaky but sturdy enough to make it through one more bus ride. The clinic is right by the bus stop, so as long as I end up plopping myself through the clinic doors, I'll be seen.

Within about a minute or two, I notice I get my strength back. Head still throbs, but at least I feel more confident about travelling.

I decide to put my earbuds back in when…

"RAIN MAN! RAAAAIN MAN!"

Oh, no. No way. Not on my watch. Also, how do they even know about that movie? Film class?

When I turn around, there are three young women taunting this young fella who's grasping a textbook against his chest and rocking his torso. All students, I presume.

"Hey, Rain Man! Way to take over class. Infodump much?"

"Look, Shirl, he's a rock star! Or a rocking chair."

"Didn't he say he wants to get a PhD? So… will that make him The Good Doctor?"

They cackle like the hags from MacBeth. I personally wish they were acting in MacBeth, so I could shout out the name of the play and bring down whatever curses await.

"Leave me alone," the guy says softly.

One of the froshes flicks her swoopy bangs and says, "Heading to the pub crawl later, loser? Gonna try reaching way out of your league again by asking my friends out? Like we would ever want to be seen hanging with Trevor, the Big Bang nerd."

"Ugh, can you even?" says another Macbeth witch. "I'd be embarrassed to be even standing next to him at a party."

Young Trevor clutches his book and rocks harder. I understand that feeling and have done similar movements myself throughout my life when The Overwhelm took hold.

PUTTING A BEE IN THEIR BONNET

"Could you imagine what people would say if they thought we liked Rain Man in that way? We'd be totally discarded pledges."

"Oh, forget about him. We need to focus on getting into that exclusive house. So, tonight, we'll hit the dance floor with some real men, then the fab-four sisters will beg us to join!"

"Yeah, exactly. We'll party till it's tomorrow!"

"Midnight is only the start of the ball, my friends!"

I smirked. This time, I felt like I had control of what would happen next. I willed that whirlwind in my core, could feel it grow as I connect with the speakers of dozens of electronic devices in the vicinity. I let my eyes fall into The Stare™ and push with all my might.

Somehow, I can boost the amplification of the musical accompaniment until the air pulsates with synthesized disco, but I draw it back just enough for the bass not to overwhelm. One by one, each of the trio began to sing, "Gimme Gimme," emoting to the full and dancing with perfect synchronicity, expressing their wish for a man after midnight. All three of them show their surprise at this sudden urge to perform, but quickly revel in it as a crowd gathers, fascinated. Once again, phones are drawn out.

The singers adore having all eyes on them.

The fella they'd been mocking stops rocking and gawks at them as if they'd collectively lost any sense.

Emerging from the growing crowd are four other perfectly coiffed and polished female students. With arms folded and expressions of disgust mixed with bafflement, they click their tongues in unison. Maybe they're the Quartet of Destiny?

"Are they for real singing to Trevor O'Hara?" asks one of them. "Isn't he the newbie weirdo genius?"

Another repulsed fashionista snarls her glossy lip. "Yeah, okay, whatever. I thought they were a good fit, but I guess they're going another way."

"Let's give them a pass on joining our house. Looks like they're more into nerds anyway. The Gamma Geeks can have 'em. They take *anyone*."

The sorority sisters bounce away, but not before shaking their heads at the trio of singers, who catch sight of their sneers. By the time the song finishes, some of the gathered horde claps, some laugh, but mostly the students are engrossed in posting the video on every platform they can find. The frosh trio panics and chases after their preferred house leaders.

Funny, those three were actually quite talented. I hope one day they wake up and use their skills for good, instead of being gross to other humans.

I want to approach the lad, but another student beats me to it. This young soul sports a slouchy purple knit hat with stripes in yellow, white, purple, and black and a massive THEY pronoun woven into it. Pink and ash blond hair poke out from under the wool. Warm brown eyes and a bright smile adorn their golden-brown features. They softly tap the guy's shoulder.

"Hi, Trevor, my name is Jody," they sign.

Suddenly, I curse myself and feel a bit ashamed for not communicating with ASL enough these past two years. I'm still able to follow though.

Trevor puts his textbook on the ground. "How did you know my name?" he signs back.

"I was in the class. You rocked it." Jody jumps, aghast, realizing their choice of words.

PUTTING A BEE IN THEIR BONNET

Trevor laughs easily though, crinkling his freckled nose and brushing away his ginger locks. "Yeah, I am a multi-purpose rocker."

Jody giggles with relief. "Anyway, I saw you sign the other day. You were on your phone. Video call?"

"Yeah. My folks and I are not Deaf, but I prefer communicating this way, to be honest. Sound and I are not always good friends."

"Cool. I am Deaf," Jody signs, "and wish there were more classes with interpreters."

Trevor's eyebrows raise. "Would you want to team up and see if we can talk to

Administration about this?"

"Cute how you think I do not already have a team."

"Crap. Sorry."

"Want to join us?"

His face beams. "Sure!"

"Got some time to go for a coffee?"

"I do!"

"Great!"

I smile. The kids are all right. At least some of them are. Hopefully the rest will learn and grow.

And here comes my bus.

What a bizarre day. I mean, I deal with ableism against Autistics all the time and try to fight back with well-crafted arguments, facts, and lived-experience education, but it just doesn't seem enough. It's as if neurotypical folks just *want* to misunderstand us, maybe visit *their* lack of empathy on us, and force us into a box not of our own making. Organizations that aren't led by us are dominating the narratives, drowning out our own voices. What if the only way for them to back off is to get their attention in ways beyond what they're used to? What would happen if we really did have superpowers? How would we use them?

I stiffen. Do I have a superpower now? Is this my origin story?

Am I suddenly faced with a great responsibility?

I ponder the events since the lightning strike while watching the scenery outside my window. Three stops before my medical clinic—situated in a residential suburb among the endless similarly designed houses—is a sprawling community centre. There's an enormous sign outside that sometimes displays health information or upcoming seminars. This afternoon it reads:

Applied Behaviour Analysis Symposium, Auditorium 1, today, 3pm.

It's 3:15 pm. I press the bell button several times and shout with fervour, "Let me off! Please let me off! I want to get off the bus!"

The driver knows me, so she hits the breaks a couple of metres past the stop and opens the door. I exit the bus. My head seems less achy for some reason.

A wind has picked up. I can feel it all around me, but not blowing against me; rather, it's holding me up, fortifying. From a nearby home, a golden sateen top sheet is freed from its clothesline. It flies through the air and lands at my feet.

I pick it up, tie it about my neck like a cape, and straighten my shoulders.

The doctor can wait. I do have a great responsibility to carry.

I saunter into the community centre, cheerfully whistling to myself and rewriting the lyrics in my head to "The Winner Takes It All."

JOY JUMPERS

BY KS PALAKOVIC

CN: Non-graphic violence, mention of blood

"Heads," Erika said.

"You always guess heads." Cherry rolled the coin between long fingers.

"That's because your coin is loaded. You like going forward more than back."

"I am deeply offended by both those insinuations, my love," Cherry said. "I'm an equal opportunity time traveler who takes our game very seriously."

"Last time you tried to see if you could get the coin to land on its side so we wouldn't have to go anywhere."

"I was tired! 1731 was exhausting, all those petticoats." Cherry tossed the coin into the air and caught it, flipping red curls out of her face. "Come on, let's just go to the future. It's better there. And you don't have to wear as many clothes."

"Heads."

Cherry rolled her eyes. "Okay, fine." She flicked the coin up, caught it, and slapped it into the back of her other hand.

It was heads.

Cherry grinned. "Guess we both win, babe. Let's get changed."

"Wait," Erika said. "Let's set up the blocker first. I don't want to forget."

"We won't forget," Cherry said. "And we won't get caught. You worry too much, it's that anxiety disorder flaring up again."

Erika dodged Cherry's peck on the cheek. "I worry exactly the right amount about this. I'm not risking an infinity in time-jumping jail because we didn't hide our trail, after we paid all that money for the blocking software."

"Alright, alright." Cherry sat down beside Erika at the console, a dark box punctuated with rhythmically blinking blue lights. "You run the program; I'll check the manual settings on our set."

They worked in silence for a few minutes, Erika typing at the console and Cherry adjusting minuscule switches and dials on a pair of metal bracelets that blinked in time with the dark box.

"You know," Cherry said, "this would go a lot faster if we'd gone with the legit models I found."

"You mean the stolen tech? And get hunted down by the Institute? No, thanks. These bracelets may be black market, but they're untraceable."

"Babe, those stuffed-up snoots have better things to do than hunt down a couple of joy jumpers. They're out there trying to optimize the moral utility of the universe, remember? Finding real villains and disasters and such."

Erika shook her head. "You know the Institute doesn't really distinguish between history's fascists and people like us. And no one thinks they'll get caught until they do. We've been jumping for over a year now, and there aren't many of us still doing this, and—"

"Hey," Cherry said, putting her pale hand on Erika's plump brown arm. "We're not gonna get caught. Okay? This blocker is top-notch, and we're smarter than a bunch of academic cops."

Erika gave her a half-smile. "Are you sure?"

"Hell yes. You're my genius girl," Cherry said, wrapping her arms around Erika's waist. "I'll keep you safe. And hey, bracelets are all set up. You almost finished?"

"Done," Erika said. "Let's roll."

■ ·■■ · ■■··■■ --- ■■■■

Laughter burst into the tiny apartment as the two girls re-entered existence there.

"Oh my god," Cherry said. "The look on that guy's face."

Erika wheezed. "I can't believe you said I was an alien."

"He totally believed it!"

"No one believes in aliens that far in the future!"

They collapsed onto the bed in a heap of giggles.

"Hey," Erika said. "Where's my prize?"

"Damn, I was hoping you'd forget," Cherry said. "Alright, I'll get started cooking. But it's gonna be mac and cheese again."

"Joke's on you," Erika said as Cherry stood up and grabbed a pot. "That's my favourite."

■ ·■■ · ■■··■■ --- ■■■■

Stars shone through the dusty window. From a distant street, a siren called out.

"Hey," Erika said. "Let's not jump tomorrow."

Cherry rolled over to face her in the small bed. "Why not?"

"I just want to hang out with you for a bit."

"Here?" Cherry said. "In a hundred square feet of boredom?"

"I'll entertain you." Erika kissed the freckles on Cherry's neck.

"Or we could go somewhere we can both be entertained," Cherry said. "Meteors at Moon Park? Berlioz in Paris? You love Paris."

Erika shifted. "I just think maybe we should take it easy on the jumping."

"Babe." Cherry looked up at the ceiling. "You're worrying again."

"Well, someone has to."

Cherry sighed and rolled back over. "Maybe I'll just go on my own tomorrow."

"What?" Erika sat up. "You promised."

Cherry didn't reply.

"Cheryl," Erika said.

"Don't call me that."

"Please tell me you won't go alone." She touched Cherry's shoulder.

"Fine." Cherry looked back at Erika. "But we're going tomorrow, right?"

"Okay," Erika said. "Yeah. We'll go."

■ ▪ ■ ▪ ■ ▪ ▪ ■ ▪ ▪ ■ ▪ ▪ ▪ ■ ▪ ■ ■

"We don't actually have to go," Cherry said. "If you don't want to."

"No, I want to." Erika laced up her boots. "I like the past. You set up the blocker for backward travel, right?"

"Of course," Cherry said. She glanced at the console while Erika looked down at her shoes, and then breathed a silent sigh of relief.

Erika was humming to herself. "I'm glad we're going. This will be fun."

"You bet it will be," Cherry said, smiling. "Now get your pretty self all ready to go."

Erika smiled back. "Yes, dear."

■ ∙■■ ∙ ■■∙∙■ ∙ ∙ ∙ ■ ■ ■■

Cherry lowered Erika onto the stony road as gently as she could. Blood glistened on the unmoving woman's face.

"Babe," Cherry said. "Babe, get up. Please get up. Erika."

In the distance, shouts drew closer. Cherry fumbled with Erika's bracelet, which fizzled and went dark. She swore.

"I'm sorry," Cherry said, a tear falling onto Erika's matted black hair. "We don't have to go anywhere tomorrow. Okay? Just get up, okay?"

Footsteps echoed on gravel, nearer and nearer.

"You're faking," Cherry said. "It's not funny. They're gonna catch us, and—"

A uniformed figure rounded the corner and entered the alleyway. "You two! Stop!"

"Leave us alone," Cherry shouted. "We aren't hurting anyone."

"You're trespassing in time," the uniform said. "And disrupting the Utilitarian Institute's work to maximize good."

Cherry spat on the ground. "Maximize my ass."

The uniform ignored this. "You know what happens next. It's not your first time, is it, Cheryl?"

Cherry looked down at Erika. "Can you just take me? And leave her out of this?"

"That's not how it works. You're both complicit."

"She's hurt," Cherry said. "She needs help."

"Time travel is a dangerous game. Come on." The uniform reached a hand down to where Cherry was crouched over Erika's body.

Cherry growled. "Time didn't hit her. You bloody uniforms did."

"You know we can't have a dark-skinned woman wandering around medieval Finland. Cheryl—"

Cherry clamped her jaw on the uniform's hand as hard as she could.

The uniform yelped and jumped back.

Cherry ripped off her bracelet and jammed it onto Erika's wrist alongside the broken one.

"I'll find you," she whispered, holding down a button. "I'll get out again, and I'll find you, and—"

Erika disappeared.

Hands closed down on Cherry's shoulders, one of them bearing a bite mark. "Time to go, Cheryl."

"I'll find you," Cherry said. "I'll—"

The uniform pressed a button, and the alley was empty once again.

■ ·■■ ·■■·-·■■ ···■■■■

Erika awoke to bright sunlight and the worst headache she'd ever had. There was blood on the pillow, and on her wrist, where two bracelets rested.

She blinked. "Cherry?"

The apartment was silent and empty.

She stood up gingerly, wincing as the room spun around her. A few feet away, blue lights blinked on the console in time with one of the bracelets. She crossed over to the dark box, her head pounding with each slow step, and looked at the program still running on it.

It took ten minutes of reading and rereading before she was convinced.

"We did everything right," she said softly. "We just got unlucky."

Carefully, she removed the blinking bracelet and set it down. She started to remove the broken one, but hesitated.

She sat back down on the bed. It felt too spacious. Her eyes fell on the dirty macaroni pot in the sink.

When the tears came, she let them, even though it made her head hurt twice as much.

And when the sunset glowed golden through the hazy window, she took a deep breath, and got to work.

■ ·■■ · ■■·-·■■ ···■■■

Cherry sat alone, eyes closed. There wasn't much to do in the time void; it was a place of nothingness, where nothing happened. The weather was eternal summer, the food was adequate, and the loneliness was unbearable.

There were others there: fellow jumpers who'd flouted the rules for fun, along with the first scientists who had discovered time travel, only to find themselves whisked away by the Institute for breaking laws that didn't yet exist. The jumpers complained often about the time laws being unfair. Cherry mostly kept to herself.

After her first decade, she'd taken up meditating. In her second, she'd stopped calling it meditating and embraced doing nothing. Some time after that, she'd stopped counting the decades.

Sometimes she thought of her old life, and her certainty that she wouldn't get caught twice—and that even if she did, she'd be able to break out again. But things were different now. She knew what she'd done.

"Cherry?"

Cherry opened her eyes. She looked down at her hands, gnarled with time she couldn't escape.

"Cherry, it's me," said Erika, placing her smooth hand on Cherry's wrinkled one. A bracelet blinked blue on the now-much-younger woman's wrist. "I'm sorry it took me so long. These things are hell to fix, and finding the right timeline…"

Cherry smiled and looked up at her. "Babe, it's been no time at all."

Erika smiled back. She pulled out a second blinking bracelet, and a coin. "Heads or tails?"

A tear slipped down Cherry's cheek. She reached up to Erika's outstretched hand and took the coin, then dropped it onto the ground at their feet. "Home."

DEATH IN THE RAIN

BY DAVE LERNER

CN: Off-screen death, mention of burns, autistic meltdown

The Level Eleven Boss *finally* dies. II'm about to start Level Twelve, but I'd better check the time first. Protection: Earth has its weekly meeting at seven pm. I think it's silly to have a mandatory meeting when more than half the team is off in Parallel D21, but Man-Tank is a stickler for the rules. I don't think he's autistic or has OCD. He just has SUHBD. Stick Up His Butt Disorder. Now, I actually am autistic, so I like the idea of following the rules and keeping to routine. But I also have ADHD, which makes following the rules and keeping to routine difficult.

You're allowed to be both.

DEATH IN THE RAIN

I check the time.

DAMMIT!

Dammit, dammit, dammit!

7:18! I'm late! Again! I got caught up in *Adventurers Against the Rorckron* and time… just got away from me.

I grab my costume and change as quickly as I can, which is nowhere quick enough. Red skintight sleeveless jumpsuit with little yellow sunbursts all over it, thick-soled yellow boots with red trim, and a red mask with yellow trim. I undo my ponytail and shake loose my dark brown hair.

I am no longer mild-mannered freelance cartoonist Tammy Trainor. Okay, "mild-mannered" might not be entirely accurate. I am no longer freelance cartoonist Tammy Trainor.

I am Reactor Woman!

Reactor Woman. My Reaction-Field can absorb any type of energy, strengthening my power. I can deflect bullets and other physical objects, as well as reach out and lift a few hundred pounds. I can sense energy in my immediate area, and if I want, I can absorb it, again strengthening my power. If I'm powered up enough I can heal from almost anything. I can fly thousands of miles an hour, slicing through the air without creating a sonic boom.

Which is good. Because I'm running late. Again.

I shove the small earpiece in my ear. "Man-Tank. Soundburst. Sorry I'm late. I'll be there in a minute or two."

"Are-Dub," says Man-Tank in my ear, using my initials, "we've been *trying* to reach you. We're not at headquarters. We'd gotten a report of strange weather in Cosmopolis. I would appreciate it if you could join us there. At your leisure." Man-Tank's a *supergenius*— he built his own super-suit. It's purple and black, only slightly bigger than he is, with a permanent scowl on the helmet which matches the near-permanent scowl on his face. He's dark-haired and incredibly good-looking, in a rough way you wouldn't expect from a *supergenius*, but he has poor social skills.

However, as I'd said I honestly don't think he's autistic (though I could be wrong). I *am* autistic, but I'm not a human computer like Raymond Babbitt in the movie "Rain Man".

"Heavy rains. Very bad. Not natural," chimes in Soundburst. "Lightning strikes. Actively killing people. At least five confirmed dead. Probably many more." Soundburst, as her name implies, has sonic powers. She can completely silence an area, or blast you with sound powerful enough to toss you across the room. She's somewhat taciturn and when she does speak, she rarely says more than absolutely necessary. I don't think she has much of a life outside of being a superhero. I don't think she wants one.

She's a tall, sexy white woman, with long, thick curly black hair. Her blue and white costume is considerably more revealing than mine. And she has more to reveal.

Me, I'm skinny. Not supermodel slender. Ribs-showing crawl-through-a-Froot-Loop, hide-behind-a-piece-of-string scrawny. My autism... causes sensitivities. Including food sensitivities. Drinking milk is like drinking phlegm. Mushrooms and olives just feel weird and wrong in my mouth. The smell of bacon makes me want to vomit. And I prefer to eat the same routine foods.

But my ADHD means I easily get bored with the same routine foods, and executive dysfunction makes it difficult to shop for groceries or to cook. And I frequently get caught up in something and forget to eat.

So I'm skinny.

DEATH IN THE RAIN

"We'll be there in a couple of minutes," Man-Tank says. "ALLEGIANCE is mobilizing, they'll probably be there within the hour. Who knows what damage could be done by then, so I hope you'll join us soon."

ALLEGIANCE. Alpha Level Law... something or other. The government's answer to the supervillain problem. They're actually pretty good, but they can be ruthless at times. They're even willing to kill, if necessary.

Superheroes don't kill. I have never killed. Not in real life, I mean. Slaying minions in *Adventurers Against the Rorckron* doesn't count. Now, there are a few good reasons for this. We're private citizens; most of us have secret identities. We have no right to the power of life and death. The public mostly loves superheroes, but they might not if we were killers and that would make our work much harder. And I know that killing can mess you up psychologically.

All that's true. But that's not the reason I don't kill. They say many autists and ADHDers have an overdeveloped sense of right and wrong; it's actually considered a disability. It's maybe one reason why I became a superhero in the first place. There is right and there is wrong. And killing is wrong. Pure and simple. It's wrong.

I hope we wrap this up before ALLEGIANCE arrives. If the villain is subdued, they'll just take them in. Nobody needs to die.

"I'll get there about the same time. I think." Cosmopolis is maybe a few hundred miles in the other direction from headquarters. I'd flown there before and knew the way. Mostly. "So who is it?"

"We're not sure," Man-Tank says. "We've narrowed it to three."

"Weather Girl. Rain Man. Storm Drain." Soundburst says.

"I'm trying to contact Carlton, but I think they're busy with something."

I recognize all three names.

Weather Girl could not control her powers. I'd helped bring her in. She's supposed to be at the Carlton facility, where they're working to help her.

I fly at top speed, my Reaction-Field shielding me from the wind. My fists open and close, open and close. My lips pop, making small "p" sounds. I stim—make small repetitive motions—even when I'm calm but more so when I'm nervous or annoyed. It relaxes me and helps me focus.

Rain Man, from what I understand, is not actually autistic. He said somewhere he'd never even heard of the movie. I've never faced him, but I hate him for his name alone. Ever since that movie came out, that's what *everyone* thinks *all* autistic people are like. He has absolutely no regard for human life. A few of the rest of my team had tossed the rest of his team in prison, but he'd slipped away.

Clouds around me, moving almost as fast as I am. Clouds never move this fast. I follow them to Cosmopolis.

Who was the third one? You can't give a ADHDer three names like that and expect her to remember them all!

I approach the city, lit up in the gathering dark. An area by the waterfront district is all covered in clouds. Raining hard. Constant lightning strikes. I hate rain. I hate lightning.

"Hey, guys! Who was the third one, again? Sorry!"

"Reactor Woman, this is important. Weath—"

"Man-Tank? Man-Tank, are you there? Soundburst?" I pour on speed.

I'm in the rain. Though my Reaction-Field deflects rain and keeps me dry the sound *constantly* drumming, the thunder so **LOUD!** My fists open and close, open and close. My lips pop pop.

DEATH IN THE RAIN

And the people! This area was mostly shut down at night, I guess. Not much traffic. But some. And car crashes, and cars and people have been struck by lightning... fires, even in the rain.

I put out a few fires as I go by, absorb a few lightning bolts. I want to help these people, but every second I delay stopping the supervillain responsible, more people die.

Tears well up, and I blink them away. My fists open and close, open and close. My lips pop pop.

Then I see it. The Protection: Earth shuttle. On its side in the middle of the street, burning. A lightning bolt must have hit it. The shuttle is built to survive lightning strikes, but there's a limit and the strike must have been more than it could take. The rear is torn open, obviously the fuel cell must have exploded.

If I'd been near it, I could have prevented the explosion, even absorbed the lightning strike. If I'd been closer. If I had been there. I should have been there.

I get close to it, absorb the flames to put them out, and fly in through the back.

I find Man-Tank and Soundburst. Man-Tank's armor is tough, but apparently not tough enough. It's all blackened and burned and I think the fuel cell (the same type as the shuttle) exploded. His suit is ripped open, exposing what's left of his body inside. He and Soundburst are burned almost beyond recognition. I know there's no chance, but I try to detect any energy in either of them. None.

LOUD! Not hitting the shuttle, but too close. The rain and the **LOUD!** and they're dead they're dead they're both dead...

I should have been there! I should have saved them! I should have died with them! I should **HAVE BEEN THERE! I-SHOULD-HAVE-FUCKING-BEEN-THERE!!!**

■ ▪ ■ ■ ▪ ■ ■ ▪ ▪ ■ ■ ▪ ▪ ▪ ■ ▪ ■ ■ ■

I look around. I'd blown off what was left of the roof. My Reaction-Field is down; rain slams down on me.

Meltdown. I had a meltdown. Yes, Reactor Woman has meltdowns. And this was a bad one. But every second I delay, more people die.

I'd never had a meltdown during a mission, though I'd had a few afterwards. I know that I couldn't choose to avoid this meltdown anymore than I could choose to avoid bleeding if I'd been stabbed.

My brain doesn't believe me.

Now, I have a few rituals I like to do after a meltdown. I'd sit in a darkened room, listen to soft music. But right now, I put my Reaction-Field back up and fly out. My fists open and close, open and close. My lips pop pop pop.

Water soaks my hair, costume, and boots. The rain hammers down. The **LOUD**! My teammates... The innocent people... so many innocent people... I make a decision.

Killing is wrong. Pure and simple. It's wrong. But maybe not this time. Maybe my autism is telling me not to kill, but I am more than my symptoms. Whoever is doing this... they're dead. I don't care if it's Weather Girl. I don't care if she can't help it. The bitch is dead.

I try to find the center of the storm. Yeah, ADHD usually means I can't pay attention to things. But it also means when something does get my attention I hyperfocus. Laser-focused. And I am more hyper focused now than I probably have ever been. My eyesight is normal, but I see more, notice more, process visual information better. The rain and the soaking and the loud have less effect on me for the moment. I'll pay for this later. But that's later.

In the distance, I see a building that is not getting rained on.

Though there are clouds over it, no rain is coming down on it.

DEATH IN THE RAIN

I land. The rooftop is completely dry. I'm literally dripping wet, leaving a small puddle.

I take a moment to appreciate the relative quiet. And I see *him*! Rain Man. Standing right in the middle. Good. I would've felt bad about killing Weather Girl, but I'd hated Rain Man before he'd murdered Man-Tank and Soundburst and so many others. A tall thin dark-haired man. His costume is black with little white lightning bolts all over it. He's facing the other way, talking on his phone. He doesn't see me.

My fists open and close, open and close. My lips pop pop pop.

I can't stomach the idea of walking in wet boots, so I float over to him. It's a video call. I don't recognize the woman he's talking to, but she's maybe mid-forties or so, and well-dressed.

"You still haven't released them," he says through gritted teeth. He wears a tight cowl that conceals the top part of his face, again black with white lightning bolts. "How many more people are you going to let die?!"

"I told you," the woman pleads. She's on speaker. "I don't have the authority myself! I'm trying to find somebod—"

"Shut up! Now I have to go somewhere with more people! Maybe then you'll listen to me!"

"Please! I ca—" I overcharge the phone's battery. The phone sparks and smokes, goes blank. I don't want any witnesses. Rain Man stares at it, taps it a few times. I pull the earpiece out of my ear, use my Reaction-Field to move it a small distance away, and send enough power through it to melt it. It records everything I say, everything it hears. And again, no witnesses.

"You should not have chosen *that* name, Rain Man!" I surprise myself. Of all things he's done, him choosing that particular nom de crime was hardly the worst. But that was what I'd said.

He turns around, drops his phone. "Who are you?" He has white lenses over the eyes of his cowl, so I can't actually see his eyes, which is okay. I prefer to avoid eye contact anyway.

"I am Reactor Woman. You! Have done! ENOUGH!"

"Enough? I'm just getting started!"

LOUD! Lightning strikes me. I absorb it so completely the rooftop beneath me isn't even scorched. More strikes. I lose count. I heal the damage from the thunderclaps, the air rushing to fill the sudden vacuum, with barely a thought. I'm so full of energy I have to shoot blasts off into the sky. "My turn."

He puts his hands up. "I surrender." He doesn't sound scared. He's smug. He has this smug little smile on his smug little face. I'm not the best at reading facial cues, but I recognize smug. I guess he figures if he surrenders, I can't hurt him, no matter how much I want to.

He figures wrong. "You don't get to surrender." I slowly move towards him.

The smugness changes to panic. He backs away from me quickly, stopping about five or six feet from the edge.

I do one of my favorite tricks: I drain just enough energy from his brain to make him pass out. I keep his energy low so he doesn't wake up. I've done this dozens—literally hundreds—of times, mostly on low-level thugs, muggers, and the like. The hard part is not to drain so much that I kill him. Not that that matters here.

The rain stops, as if a faucet has just been shut off. The clouds remain, but off in the distance the additional clouds that were coming in now stop and slowly dissipate. The clouds over me start to break up. A ray of sun hits me.

What to do what to do what to do? No witnesses, I can make up my own story afterwards. People will believe me. And Rain Man has done so much evil I doubt anyone will really care.

I could blast him. I'm still so charged I can barely contain it. I could finish draining him. I could just toss him off the roof.

A part of me says killing is wrong. But that's just my autism and ADHD. I make my own fucking choices!

I am autistic. I am an ADHDer. I am super-powered. I am a superhero. I am a member of Protection: Earth.

And I am more than that. I am a woman. I am an American. I am a freelance cartoonist. I am a video-gamer. I am an Adventurer against the *Rorckron*.

I am all of these things, and more. No one individual thing defines me. But all of these things, all the things I am, make up who I am, and guide who I will become.

I am a person who knows right from wrong. I can freely choose if I do right or if I do wrong.

And I made my choice here.

I used my Reaction-Field to lift Rain Man up and I kept him floating with me, unconscious, while I helped as many people as I could, until I was able to turn him over to ALLEGIANCE.

Then I found a quiet corner and had the worst meltdown I'd ever had.

GRANNY SMITH

BY POLLY ORR

Five years ago, Granny Smith was the only mature student enrolled at The Academy. Cape Construction 101 was a unique experience. While all the young superhero wannabes swapped swatches of latex in sexy shades of red, Granny Smith set up shop in the far-left corner with a steady click, click, click of her knitting needles. As someone who lived in the north, it wasn't practical to be traipsing about in a next-to-nothing costume. She needed a few industrious layers of wool and fleece—with some macrame flair—to swaddle her bod against eight long months of winter.

Despite what her peers may have thought, she wasn't fully abandoning fashionability; her entire life, her outfits honoured a singular eye-popping colour palette. From the hues of fresh spring buds to perfectly ripe key limes, dayglo greens put a pep in her step making more than a neighbour or two burst into smiles. What the trees lacked in green for most of the year, Granny Smith readily made up for.

With nimble, well-trained fingers, Granny's garment construction was immaculate. Years later, as large tufts of snow toppled from the sky, the only wear and tear her superhero outfit endured was a bit of a fray along the bottom edge of her cape. As old age progressed, she lost an inch of height here and there and gained it 'round the middle. Yet her midnight prowling never slowed. Long after others had tucked into bed, she was out protecting the streets.

Tonight, was no different. She wasn't far from home, just a block or two away from her cozy bed. Just as she started to consider whether Sprightly would agree that there was a good enough reason for her to be out of that cozy bed, the air began to buzz with the sound of an alarmingly large insect. Granny smiled, searching the sky for her faerie friend, as a small creature with swishy blue hair and six perfectly symmetrical wings materialized inches from Granny's nose.

"Are you okay Granny? Are you breathing? Are you hurt? Did you—"

"Sprightly. I am fine." Granny leaned back, scooting her butt even further down into the snow. "I didn't fall over. I'm just pausing to enjoy the view." Tipping her head back, she let her vision fill with hundreds of tiny white dancers falling from the sky.

Sprightly flitted around her once more and, satisfied with his assessment, settled into the nook just in front of the bulbous bun atop her head.

"Well Granny, I'm glad you're not asleep on the job. But I am curious. Why are you out here? In the dark? Sitting in the snow?"

"Well you know…" She peered sheepishly off into the distance while patting the top of the snow playfully. "I'm preparing to respond to a 402."

"A 402? Are you kidding me? Granny, you know that's not really superhero stuff. They've got firefighters and—"

"Shush." Scooping Sprightly off her head she placed him straight in front of her stare. "You know I love cats. The neighbours toodled off for a week. No one really asked me. I just happened to notice Jeffery was up there again."

All eyes shifted up to the edge of the three-story house. Barely visible in the stormy night was a faint smudge of movement. Almost mistakable for the howl of the wind, a feebler noise could be heard. Only three months into the world, Jeffery the cat had been on an awful lot of adventures. Most of them were great good fun on the way up, and terrifying once looking down.

Sprightly stared at Granny, cautious about what to say next. "Are you…up for this?"

Without missing a beat, Granny Smith was back on her feet, shuffling around to the back of the yard, tossing open a heavy tin door. Rummaging through the shed, she huffed over her shoulder, "Can you get Phyllis here?"

"You know she's from the sunshine realm-right? Like eternal glorious rainbow mists of delight and all that? I don't think her unicorn sensibilities are ready for winter."

"You say winter, I say winter wonderland! Now off you go, you little scamp."

Sprightly gave a nod and disappeared into the ethers, the space in between realms where he could call on Phyllis. Her aura connected with his immediately, and they buzzed away about Granny's shenanigans.

"A 402? Seriously? Again? I'm on my way."

As soon as Sprightly had popped away to grab Phyllis, Granny wasted no time advancing her adventure. In the back of the shed was just what she was looking for. Unpinning the buttons on top of her mitts to get a better grip, she began to drag the ladder across the lawn. Making deep gashes in the snow as she trudged forward, every few yards she dropped the ladder and plunged into the snow to catch her breath.

Little aches and pains jittered around inside as her deep inhales turned to clouds of visible breath around her face. She felt like a winter dragon at that moment- breathing ice instead of fire.

A lot of her peers at the Academy had spent many months labouring over which powers they wanted to develop. The first two years were introductory superhero classes, everyone pretty much took the same ones—Cape Construction, Fundamentals of Flying, Super Strength Training and Decoding the Big Book of Quests—before getting split off depending on the element they chose to develop their powers in.

Granny took off her gloves and wiggled her fingers until a small flame erupted in her palm. There was no doubt in her mind that fire was the way to go. Not only was it beneficial for saving the day, but the warm emanations often took the edge off her arthritis on stiffer days.

Feeling the movement return to her fingers, with one last heave-ho the ladder was now beneath the window. Knowing that Sprightly and Phyllis would want her to wait for their return before climbing up, she did a quick head-to-toe scan to determine if she was steady enough to go on her own.

She paid the most attention to her chest, searching for any sharp palpitation or shortness of breath. Her hands felt steady and her mind clear. As she was prone to anxiety, The Academy had assigned her Sprightly as her support spirit. They had a wonderfully nurturing bond, and he often knew just the right way to help co-regulate her nervous system when flare-ups occurred.

In this moment she felt calm and centred.

Flipping her mitten flaps back over so her fingers wouldn't freeze to the metal rungs, she started her ascent. Halfway to the top, another short pause to rest. Out of breath, but still no anxiety. This was a task she was old hat at.

When she was three rungs from the top, Jeffrey started yowling excitedly. The rascally black furball recognized Granny Smith immediately. Dashing forward, he let her scoop him up and place him into her oversized pocket. (Some kids in her class didn't put pockets in their costumes at all. Absolute fools).

Mindful to put him in her left pocket, she plunged her hand deep into the right one, which had been enchanted by wizard friend to have infinite space inside of it, and pulled out a headlamp to protect against the deepening darkness. The space was great for fitting all the snacks, meds, and extra pairs of mitts she required throughout the day, but if the cat got inside there was no telling how long it would take to find him.

Balancing the weight of the kitty in her pocket, and the lantern in her hand, Granny carefully descended the ladder until she reached the top floor window. Almost in the clear, all she needed to do was lean over and release Jeffery back inside. The Problem arose when she tried to back out.

Sprightly and Phyllis popped back from The Other Realm to the sight of Granny Smith's tiny boots flailing outside the window, her many layers of warmth wedging her firmly into the windowsill. Moving rapidly into action, Sprightly gave her tush a firm push. Her layers now provided cushioning as she made a gentle roll onto the bedroom floor.

Granny held up a hand in an attempt to stop the barrage of concern. "Now, now small one, you just happened to pop in for the last five percent of the mission when 95% was smooth and hunkydory. Let's get on home now and we can light the fire and have a cup of tea." Sprightly's mouth opened but before he could interject, Granny assured him that this time, she would take the front door.

■ ■ ■ ■ ■ ■ ■ ■ ■ ■ ■ ■ ■ ■ ■ ■ ■ ■ ■

Home safe and sound, Granny shuffled about attending to her nightly routine. With one pot of sweet floral tea simmering for her guests, she took out a separate large mug for her brew— an outlandishly bright concoction, the cayenne pepper, ginger, and turmeric helped ease her inflammation. After her little jaunt up and down the ladder, her knees were tight balls of pain.

But she knew they'd have been worse if she'd tried to fly. Flashing back to her flying classes, she'd taken great delight in practicing the deep squats that were required to ground yourself before takeoff. It started with belly breaths bringing energy up into the heart center, then surging energy down into the ground, and drawing the earth's energy back up again. When enough momentum is built, you would bend down until your butt almost touched your heels, then jump to lift off.

Before becoming a superhero, Granny Smith was a powerful herbalist, and she knew many potent remedies for almost any ache or pain. But the amount of powerful energy that coursed through your legs during take-off really did a number on you. Superheroes were already known for getting knee issues much earlier than the general population, and it didn't help the matter that she'd started at The Academy when she was seventy-three. Her mind flashed back to her slow climb up the ladder to rescue Jeffery. If she'd still had the knees for flying, this would have only taken 30 seconds. In. Out. No sending Sprightly into a fretting frenzy. But she knew in her heart when she started the Academy that this time would come, and she'd already resolved to keep being a force for good no matter what accommodations it took.

After taking three big gulps of her soothing remedy, Granny Smith reminded herself she was not only powerful, but she was also clever. And she felt proud to have found and managed an old school ladder rescue- even as it got a little touch and go at the window.

Sprightly popped Granny out of her absorption as he flickered into the room and nestled on her head, waiting for his dollhouse teacup to be filled with a few drops of tea. "Granny-what's that smell?" Scanning the room, he zeroed in on a black circle seared into the Formica countertop.

"Oh, no worries, dear. I was just re-warming a cup of tea with my laser vision. My cataracts throw off my aim some days. But I got it on the second go."

Sprightly slid his slender fingers over the burn mark. Wiping the charcoal residue onto his tunic he buzzed into the living room to join the meeting. A muffled whinny prompted Granny to push up the bottom half of her window so Phyllis could put her head through. Phyllis eyed the gap suspiciously, making sure to go horn first. The warm air inside the room melted the snowflakes on her short pearly hair and the glow from the fireplace glinted off her lavender eyes. Granny sauntered over and gave a gentle pat to the sensitive spot beneath her horn.

"I know unicorns don't have snow in your realm- so I made you these." From the depths of her knitting bag, she pulled up two pairs of neon pink knee socks with little leather pads stitched to the bottom. With a wide-eyed stare that could have been horror or delight, Phyllis accepted them. Sprightly zipped through the window and with all his might helped roll up the socks to their full forty-inch glory.

"Well, that's enough exercise for the week," Sprightly wheezed as he flopped back onto the carpet.

Phyllis heaved something long and slender over the windowsill. "I've got something for you too."

Sprightly caught sight of it and with a huff popped away into The Other Realm. His dramatic exit was quickly overshadowed by the presence of the gift. Granny's hand trembled slightly as it caressed the long steel shaft of the sword known as *The Dragon Slayer*. Phyllis had stopped at the Quest Bureau to grab the gear they needed for their next mission, which included this magnificent blade.

Normally after graduation from The Academy and the allocation of superpowers, such archaic technology was not needed. But dragons were ancient beasts, often immune to the slings of modern arrows. Laser vision and fireballs felt more like a massage to such a creature.

As someone who had elected for fire powers, Granny had always felt some affinity towards dragons. But she didn't feel comfortable telling the Quest Bureau she didn't want to go. At seventy-seven years old, they were always sniffing around for a reason to retire you.

"There's also this." Phyllis passed along a bag filled with thick layers of fireproof material.

"Harumph. Well, it doesn't exactly match my outfit."

"Granny, the only things that match your outfits are parrots and kiwis."

"Well, you *would* be trying to think of tropical things right now. Why don't you come around the front and I'll let you in. You can warm up by the fireplace and sleep. We'll leave in the morning."

■ ·■■ · ■■··■ · ··· ■■■■

Late next morning, as Granny was tying on the last of her fire gear, Sprightly still hadn't returned from The Other Realm. Granny was about to ask Phyllis to go searching when the spirit zapped in and perched on her knee.

"Ready to go, pipsqueak?"

"You know you're my girl Granny. I'd do anything for you. But I don't actually... *believe* in dragon hunting."

Granny reeled back almost booting Sprightly into the air. "What? Are you trying to get me exiled from The Academy too? You're my support spirit! You're supposed to help keep me calm and centred and...and..." Gasping for air, her eyes bulged as she clutched her knees. Sprightly dashed over and put his small forehead right against her third eye. Their breath came into unison and Granny calmed.

"I studied them in charm school," Sprightly began again just above a whisper "I'm actually pretty fluent in Dragon Tongue. It's a beautiful language. They have very sensitive scales all along their forehead and jaw. They basically communicate through elaborate nuzzles. You can simulate the phrases in a basic way by touching them in the correct patterns with your hands. And if you just—"

"Of course," Granny interjected roughly. "You've got to get an inch from their fangs to say hello. How convenient."

An awkward silence extended as Sprightly slowly circled and Granny fiddled with a loose piece of yarn at the end of her cloak. "Well. I'm going."

"Fine. Then you better take this. Put it in your special pocket." Barely strong enough to lift it from the ground, Sprightly heaved an overstuffed bag onto the countertop. Inside were reams of freshly picked chamomile, lavender, and motherwort, hand-drawn note cards with several breathing techniques and a handful of fidget toys. "I'm not going to a spa you know- I'm going to slay a dragon!"

"Exactly! And if your anxiety comes on in the process…" He paused to gain composure and bring his voice back to even. "We've worked together a long time. I know these are helpful. Please. Just take it."

■ ∙■ ■ ∙ ■ ■∙∙ ∙ ■ ■ ∙ ∙ ∙ ■ ■ ■ ■ ■

Preoccupied by Sprightly's absence, the journey to the dragon's cave came and went in a blur. As they traversed into The Other Realm, Granny barely heard Phyllis as the unicorn expounded on their mission. They had been sending their villagers to the cave over the years… something, something about the bureaucratic process… the village wanted a permanent superhero…sending a temp to slay the dragon rather than protect full-time cuts down on admin costs. Something, something about values and duty.

Rolling up to the cave, Granny's head was far away from the dragon-slaying protocols she'd learned in school as she marched in yelling, "HEY THERE SCUZZY SCALEY CREEP! HERE I COME!"

A thunderous boom shook the entire cave. Granny tumbled to the ground. Increasingly disoriented, piercing booms brought down shards of boulder all around her. In the far-off distance, she heard Phyllis calling out, then silence. Granny could no longer see the light of day and The entrance was fully blocked.

A sharp pain pierced her temple but a quick fumble with her hands revealed no external wound. Doubled over from a twin stab of pain in her stomach, her breath became erratic. Too dark to see, her hands plunged into her endless pocket, but her mind was not clear enough to make sense of the shapes she found within it. As she descended into her panic attack the dragon sharing the dark with her loomed terrifyingly large at an unknown distance.

Dizziness in full swing, she lurched towards the edge of the cave, slinking down to the ground, pressing her forehead against cool earth. Something felt strange about this sudden surge of anxiety. She'd always had her triggers, but she'd walked a long journey with them and knew them well. Breathing as fully as she could into her belly, she found it odd that the anxiety came now.

She had been in many perilous situations. Quests often took her to the cusp of danger, but this was when she got the most focused and clear. Although it had taken deep work with Sprightly and her teachers, her acute sensitivity to danger and her inner states eventually became an ally. Anxiety often came *before* the danger— unless it was garbage day, grocery day and laundry day all at once, then it was a non-stop ride until Sprightly tucked her into bed with tea. The intense inner vibrations pre-battle helped her be sharp and sure. Reassuring the inner waves of contraction that any uncertainty and peril would be well met, her stalwart strength and strategy always showed up to ease the waves. But anxiety arriving now? In the middle of battle? This was strange.

The cave had not shaken in a few minutes. She guessed the dragon had stopped moving. There was a burning in her palms as if her body wanted her to make a fireball appear, but she feared the risk of losing the darkness which protected her position.

Yet when she thought of calling forth the flame, her breathing became calmer, so she tried. As she held the flame in her palms, her spine became energized and straightened. Slipping her shoes off and placing her feet on the earth, she steadied. Slowly peering out she began to take a cursory glance around the cave.

Curled into a ball on the far side of the cave was the dragon. The enormous beast had nostrils Granny could crawl inside and phenomenally sharp barbs down its back and tail. But what took her most by surprise was its eyes.

Large sinewy strands cross-hatched both sockets, sealing them shut with scar tissue and callouses. Fully healed, they would have come from a long-ago battle and meant one thing for sure- the dragon could no longer see.

A soft popping noise almost made Granny cry out but the touch of small familiar hands on her cheek stopped her.

In a tiny whispering voice, Sprightly urged, "Don't move. Phyllis called me as soon as you got trapped. I'm going to go talk to her."

"Her?"

"Yes, her. You can tell by the slight curl at the end of her horns." Sprightly was so small and delicate, the dragon was not likely to hear him coming. A few minutes later there were some soft groans from the dark, mournful but not dangerous. Sprightly returned with the news.

"She was blinded by the first villager who came to her cave, many generations ago." There was an emotional rasp in his voice as he continued. "She never bothered anyone, and lived here peacefully for many years, but then they came and blinded her. When others come, she gets very afraid, and her thrashing bumps things around. She doesn't mean to hurt no one. She just gets scared and…and…"

Granny Smith scooped up the distraught Sprightly and cradled him, his small tears like a misty morning on her fingertips.

In the gentlest voice possible Granny leaned over and shared, "As soon as I got in here, even before it started caving in, I got real panicky. Maybe the worst anxiety I've ever felt. It had a different message than usual. Urgent. It wanted me…to stop."

In the dark, two points of red lit up as Granny's laser eyes briefly flashed. "I'm a fire creature too. Some part of me knew I didn't want to hurt this dragon. Sprightly, can you give her a message for me?"

Phyllis paced back and forth nervously on the other side of the rubble. She bucked and brayed as some large stones started to shift. Ready to charge with fierce solidarity for her trapped friends, she stopped short as she saw Granny Smith emerge sitting calmly atop the dragon's head.

■ ·■■ ·■■·¯■■ ···■■■■■

"So…let me get this straight," Phyllis starts. "Granny Smith, you are taking the dragon home with you?"

"Yes, dearie. That suits me just fine. Sprightly here has taught me how to sign left, right, up, and down, so we should be able to get home nice and quickly. Although we'll all have more Dragon Tongue to learn soon enough!"

"You know they'll expel you from Academy alumni perks for this"

"Academy shmademy. This is a quest *I* want to do." Motioning to Sprightly she asks for help translating and then tells the dragon,

"I'll be your eyes; you be my wings."

"No changing your mind is there?" Phyllis asks.

"Nope," Granny replies.

Sprightly beams.

"Phyllis, do you think we could fit a drill bit onto your horn? I think we're going to need to put an extension on our fence for our sweet new friend."

Mounting the dragon once more, Granny fishes out a long stick and a hearty kettle from the depths of her never-ending pocket along with a bit of rope. After her hands slip a few times, Sprightly pops over to help tie the kettle to the end of the pole. She swoops the kettle over the scaley forehead, and it lands just in front of the dragon's elongated nose. Gently, she moves her hands across the dragon's forehead in the newly learned pattern. In response, a little snort and a small stream of flames lick the bottom of the kettle.

"She wants me to tell you her name is Bedelia," Sprightly offers.

"Wonderful Bedelia. You're doing just wonderful. Just a few more hours and we'll all be home."

THE GLAUC BITCHES

BY MELISSA YI

CN: Animal abuse

"I'm scared." Priya pitched backwards in Suzy's grandmother's rocking chair, her feet nearly upsetting the mug of hot chocolate on the coffee table in front of her.

"Everyone gets scared," said Suzy, slipping a coaster under the hot chocolate and discreetly withdrawing the mug six inches from the edge.

"Not me!" Tantum shifted the entire table a foot away from the rocking chair. "I'm a superhero! And you could be too, Priya."

Priya's hand fisted around her mug's handle. "Who'd want a hero who's going blind?"

Tantum glared at her. "First of all, you're not blind. You have glaucoma. Big deal."

"I'm only 38. The ophthalmologist said she usually sees patients in her 80s. Kind of a big deal."

"You can still see, right?"

"Right," said Priya, "but I already have a bit of decreased vision in my right eye, maybe because I got a field hockey stick to it when I was 17—"

"Don't beat yourself up about it," said Suzy, scooping the maraschino cherry out of her own cocktail, which was apparently called a Corpse Reviver #2 . "A guy accidentally punched me in the eye during sex. Did that contribute to my glaucoma at age 62? So what?"

Priya and Tantum stared at Suzy for a second.

"No slut-shaming, remember?" Suzy popped the cherry into her mouth and chewed vigorously.

"No slut-shaming," Tantum agreed slowly, glancing down at her right big toenail, which had bored a hole through the fluffy pink sock. She hadn't said her age, but Priya guessed she was in her 50s.

Priya covered Suzy's shoulder with her hand and glanced away from the hole-y sock, even though Tantum didn't seem to embarrass easily. "Never."

"On the upside," said Tantum, setting her beer down on the table, "people who get glaucoma early tend to develop superpowers. You may not have noticed because you were so busy panicking-. Which is fine. You're the youngest of our group, anyway. But it's time for your first secret mission."

"What if I'm not a superhero, and I just have bad eyes?" Priya asked.

"Suzy and I will bail you out."

"Okay. What are your superpowers?" Priya struggled not to put air quotes around the words. She didn't want to offend Tantum. The woman was kind of scary, almost a foot taller than her, with biceps as big as a tree trunk.

Tantum grinned. "You'll find out. Now our mission. Time to save the dogs!"

"Why do the dogs need rescuing?" Priya asked.

"Bad ex," said Tantum. "They broke up. Thom kicked Chanel out and kept all three dogs, even though she paid for half of them and she's the one who really loves them."

"Yikes. I hear custody cases are the hardest. It also means we'd have to carry out one dog each," said Priya.

"Watch these videos where Chanel explains why she couldn't fight him, and how he threatens the dogs," said Tantum cheerfully.

Three videos later, Priya said, "I'm in."

"No time like the present," said Tantum. "It's only five miles s from here. Let's go."

Ugh. Priya took a few minutes to borrow some black clothes ("Good job I saved some of my daughter's things," said Suzy). As a final touch, Priya donned gloves, since she had no desire to leave her fingerprints anywhere. Then she took a deep breath and set into Vermont's November night to save the doggies.

On the ride over in the SUV, which smelled like gym bags and managed to shed dog hair on her trousers already, Priya asked from the back seat, "Should we report him to the police instead?"

Suzy hit the gas pedal while Tantum twisted around to lecture Priya from the passenger seat. "The police won't do anything for animals. We'd have to talk to animal control, and they're overwhelmed with pandemic puppies and cats right now. They sent an animal control officer over to ring Thom's doorbell, but ..."

"Thom wasn't home. He's never home. Big businessman, you know?" Suzy rolled her eyes and braked at a red light.

"Are they big dogs?" Priya asked. Chanel's videos hadn't specified.

"One big golden retriever mix, Chloe. One little terrier, Atlas, that he's been keeping in a cage, as far as we know. And one old dog, Eugenia. With skin issues. She's terrified he'll hurt Eugenia."

Suzy pulled up to the sidewalk and cut the engine while Tantum tucked something dark into her leg holster.

"What's that?" asked Priya.

"My Glock," said Tantum.

"Oh no! I've never been around a gun before!" Priya nearly leaped out of the car.

Tantum laughed. "You're from Toronto, right? The big city Canadians can't handle guns. No problem here in Burlington. We don't have any gun permit laws in Vermont."

"Forget about the gun," said Suzy, slamming her own door shut. "Think about the dogs. Thom's using them to hurt her. I know men like this. They get off on control."

Tantum nodded and shouldered a backpack as she stepped out of her car and locked it. "I guarantee he's congratulating himself right now about how he got away with this. Well, don't worry, doggies! Here come the glaucoma bitches. I'm starting to get tunnel vision, but I can still rule the world"

"And you're still allowed to drive and shoot?" Priya asked.

"I can move my head to see if I need to," said Tantum. "Suzy has almost full vision, like you."

Priya sighed, wondering why they'd included her, but Chanel's videos kept her locked in place. "What do you need me for?"

"Well, you're the youngest and strongest. You can help carry the big dog."

Priya gulped. "Excuse me?"

"Chanel sent pictures of Chloe hiding in a corner. Chloe may not want to come out. That's where you come in!"

"Please tell me Chloe likes treats."

"She does, but she may be too scared to come to us."

"I'm good with dogs," said Suzy.

"Why doesn't Chanel join us?" Priya asked. "The dogs will come to her. She's the one who can bust them out."

"He's got cameras on his property. If Chanel gets caught, she'll do time and she'll never get the dogs back. Plus she doesn't have glaucoma, right?"

"I keep wondering how glaucoma is supposed to be an advantage."

Tantum sighed and circled back to Priya, forgetting Thom's house for a moment. "Let me make it real simple for you. When you look at pictures of crones, what do you see?"

"Uh, black cloaks, big noses with a wart, rheumy eyes?"

Tantum snapped her fingers. "See, that's what no one ever told you. Losing your vision early isn't a death sentence. It's actually a gateway into a bigger power. You just don't know it yet."

Suzy shook her head at Tantum. "We can't force her to understand. Darling, your superpowers will come out under stress. This is the perfect opportunity for you. Save three dogs and get those powers going!" She patted Priya's hand. "The powers are proportionate to losing your sight, so if you're just starting to lose it, you're a newb and can't count on much power. Tantum's the strongest."

Tantum flexed her biceps under her jacket and stuck out her tongue.

Priya exhaled. She knew she should say no, stay home, drink tea, and deal with the invasive lady beetles crowding her apartment ceiling.

Instead, they fell silent and climbed the hill toward Thom's house, to save Chanel's dogs.

After five minutes of huffing, Priya asked, "Why didn't you park closer? You didn't mention the hill."

"Security cameras."

"We haven't thought this through. You said that one dog is gentle but may not come to us because we're strangers and she's given up hope."

"Chloe," said Suzy.

"Right. Who are the two others?"

"Well, you can pick up Atlas with one hand. I even brought a backpack for him." Tantum tapped one black strap.

"There's a catch, I know there is," said Priya.

"Chanel thinks Atlas is being kept in a cage that's too small for him to stand up all the way. He might get claustrophobic and fight the backpack, or even bite us."

"Ughhhhhhhh!" Priya gripped the roots of her own hair.

"Right. We're not sure what's happening to the third dog, Eugenia. She's a love, but very old and has skin allergies that he never liked taking care of. Eugenia hasn't been to the vet recently."

"Is she big too? You didn't mention her size."

"The biggest, but skinny. Might be losing her fur," Tantum admitted.

"And twelve years old," said Suzy.

Tantum glared at her.

"What? Had to be said." Suzy brushed a few dog hairs off her lap.

"So we have three imprisoned dogs with mental, physical, and possible untreated skin conditions that we have to steal back and carry down a hill," said Priya. "This is going to take a miracle."

"Can you dream up any more noble cause for the glauc bitches?" Tantum demanded.

"No," said Priya.

"All right, then." Tantum marched up the side of the hill, and slid toward the trees, away from the driveway.

"Wait. We need a plan."

But Tantum seemed to disappear into the night sky. Not blend into it, but straight up disappear. Priya whirled to stare at Suzy.

"That's one of her superpowers," said Suzy. "She can merge with the darkness."

"And turn invisible? I wish you'd told me that before!"

"Showing works better than telling. Now hush. I don't know if his cameras record sound as well as visuals."

Priya hushed up and pulled the hoodie over her eyes. She couldn't merge with the night, no matter how much she tried. She signaled to Suzy, pointing down at the ground next to her.

Suzy nodded. Yes, she'd stay with Priya the newbie, at least for now.

Priya exhaled quietly in relief. Two people might be easier for the cameras to track than one, but she needed a friend right now, just like those poor dogs.

They inched their way to the house, an impressive two-story structure with a peaked roof. Now Priya wondered how they'd find the dogs.

Suzy silently pointed to the garage, and Priya nodded, matching the building to Chanel's videos. A man like that wouldn't allow the dogs to sully his castle. They could freeze overnight, and he wouldn't care. He could have tied them to a line outside except the neighbours might complain about barking.

This way, he could imprison them and torture them without so many people witnessing the fact.

Tantum reappeared and signaled that she hadn't been able to break open the front garage door, but she opened and closed her hands several times: she'd heard barking.

Priya nodded in understanding. At least one dog was alive and trapped in the garage. A mixed blessing as the trio approached the front door of the garage, sealed shut now to keep the dogs and any remaining car inside.

Priya tiptoed to the left and around the building and found one locked door at the back. Presumably a third door inside the garage linked it to the house.

Suzy hummed under her breath. Priya turned to motion her to stop, but then she realized something strange. Suzy had … not disappeared, but shrunk. The woman dwindled, growing shorter and shorter.

Priya bit back a scream as Suzy's body spread out at the same time. She morphed sideways, losing her head, her face to become a blob that wore clothes, before the clothes themselves hit the ground. Tantum materialized and scooped the clothes up, dropping them in her backpack.

Then Tantum held up the flap built into the back door.

Thing-that-was-Suzy oozed under the door frame and into the garage before reforming.

What the actual fuck, Priya wanted to say, but bit back. She squeezed her eyes shut, praying for some sort of superpower herself, but all she could feel was her own panicked heartbeat.

Then Priya heard barking, faint but unmistakable, from more than one dog.

Her heart sang. These brilliant women had located the dogs.

Priya heard the sound of a bolt being thrown from the inside, and the garage's back door opened, revealing a naked and unashamed Suzy who'd already turned away to reach the first dog.

Eugenia shivered and shook in a cage near the door.

"It's okay darling," Priya whispered, before she stopped herself from speaking or drawing more attention to herself. At least one black camera stood directly above her head to take in anyone who came through the front door, another focused on the room including herself, so Priya kept her head averted but stretched her hand toward the poor black and white dog with her missing and matted fur.

Eugenia shied away from her.

Priya unlatched the cage and held out her hand.

The dog barked once, showing her teeth.

Priya swore under her breath.

Meanwhile, Tantum rattled Atlas's cage bars loudly, trying to free him, before giving up and dumping the entire cage in her backpack. A tiny dog's yelp was the only response before Tantum moved to help Suzy with Chloe.

Suzy stood naked next to Chloe, still not a bit bothered by her own nudity, as she whispered gently to the golden retriever mix.

"It's okay, sweet darling, I've got you. No one will ever hurt you." The garage lights flashed on above them.

The three women froze. Eugenia barked sharply, then cowered as if her own voice had frightened her.

They heard the wheels of a car roaring up the driveway.

"Holy fucking shit," said Tantum, pressing against the wall instead of disappearing.

Because the lights were on, realized Priya. Tantum's ability to merge with the shadows didn't work within this well-lit garage.

"Run," said Priya.

"I'm not leaving my glauc bitches," Tantum muttered, but with less bravado than before.

"Better you save one dog," said Suzy, who'd started to search for her clothes. Tantum pointed to the front left corner with a shaking finger right before Priya doused the lights by cutting the light switch.

The women plastered themselves against the walls as the garage door opened.

Priya couldn't do anything about the headlights, or the way the littlest dog—Atlas—barked from the depths of the backpack, but at least the car didn't hit them.

Thom stepped out and slammed his car door shut. "How're my bitches today?"

He had a nice voice, Priya would give him that. Smooth and sweet-sounding. But Eugenia quivered herself against the bars of her cage, not fooled.

Thom paused, trying to work the lights. "What the—" *Run, Tantum!* Priya thought. *Take Atlas!*

But she knew Tantum wouldn't. She wouldn't abandon her other glauc bitches.

Time for my superpower, Priya told herself.

Nothing happened. How were you supposed to manifest a superpower you didn't know you had? Priya did switch on her phone to record audio, just in case.

"C'mon, bitches. I talked to your mommy today. She cried nice fat tears for me. I'll have her begging for me soon. I just need some more pathetic pictures of my poor little doggies and mommy will come right home with her tail between her legs."

Bingo. One incriminating recording automatically uploaded to the cloud. Would that be enough?

Thom turned on his phone, catching Priya in the ambient light. "What the—"

He punched buttons on his phone to call 911.

Tantum tackled him from behind, aided by the darkness but hampered by her dog-filled backpack.

Thom donkey-kicked her, his leg lashing backward. Tantum yelped with pain, and he lit her face up with the phone, hampering her superpower.

"You broke into my house! Kind of old for a robber, aren't you?"

Tantum's arms flashed, and she pointed her gun at him, steadying it with both hands. "Screw you." She looked like she knew what she was doing, but Priya bit her lip. Tantum had the worst vision out of them all. She could easily shoot Priya or Suzy or one of the dogs, especially if Thom moved to her periphery.

Thom lunged forward. Tantum squeezed the trigger but hit the garage wall, and after a tussle too quick for Priya to understand, Thom seized the gun. "Why, look what I got here."

"Run!" Tantum shouted at them, but Suzy smiled and shifted instead. Even though Priya started toward the back door herself, she peeked over her shoulder to watch Suzy morph, her features melting, her body collapsing in on itself, reminding Priya of the Swamp Thing, no, like sheer globules of fat, an entire mountain of fat sliding toward Thom.

"Get away from me!" Thom fired the gun at Suzy's mass.

Priya snarled and leapt at Thom.

Wait, what?

No, really. Jumping, snarling, and biting his arm, taking down his gun arm so his aim sprayed a bullet into the back wall, then the wall shared with his own house.

"You bitch!" Thom shrieked, but Priya could barely hear him above her own barking, her ears partly deafened by the bullets firing.

Then Priya's teeth sank satisfyingly into Thom's flesh, her teeth clicking closed between the bones of his forearm.

He screamed, wordless now, while she wrestled him off-balance. He slipped suddenly on Suzy's grease, which had miraculously avoided Priya's own four dancing paws.

Thom landed with an audible crack on his elbow, the gun skittering across the floor.

Tantum snatched back the gun and pressed it to the man's head. "Don't you fucking move."

Priya snapped back into her human form, her heart thundering. She'd always heard that shifting was painful through books and movies, but instead, she felt exhilarated. She could taste his blood in her mouth. She could have splintered his bones with her teeth!

With her adrenaline still boiling, Priya ripped open the two bigger dogs' cages and raged at them to go, go, go!

The dogs chased Priya down the driveway now, barking, caught up in the frenzy and bloodlust. Even tiny Atlas yapped from the backpack as if he wanted to join in.

"Hold him!" Tantum called.

Suzy obediently wrapped herself around the rest of Thom's body, seeping into his mouth and nostrils, choking him while Priya cleared the hill and darted back into the car with both Eugenia and Chloe. Priya urged them into the back seat, ordering them to be quiet.

They cocked their heads and seemed to listen. They barked twice, almost as if to say, "Yes, ma'am!" before they fell silent, eyes shining.

Priya grinned back at them, revealing her still-bloody teeth as she clambered into the driver's seat.

Tantum rushed into the passenger seat, shoving her backpack, and therefore Atlas, between her feet, before slamming and locking the door. "Go, go, go!" "Suzy," said Priya.

"We'd never leave a glauc bitch behind," said Tantum, who managed to spring Atlas from the cage into her lap. She tossed the backpack under Eugenia's seat seconds before Suzy oozed beside Chloe into the back seat through the cracks in the door.

"And that's a wrap!" Tantum shouted as Priya threw the SUV into reverse.

Thom stood in the driveway, screaming at his cell phone. Then he gritted his teeth and splinted his bad arm against his side as he pounded toward them, but he was no match for a car accelerating into the night.

"He fell over!" Tantum reported gleefully. "On his bad arm! I bet the neighbours are filming him as we speak."

"They might be filming your car too," Priya pointed out, but she felt so good that she rolled down the window and ululated with joy.

The dogs howled in agreement.

"We'll bring you back to your mommy," Suzy assured the dogs, patting them between grabbing crucial bits of clothing. Somehow, she managed her underwear despite her seatbelt and two big dogs crowding two thirds of the back seat .

"Will he find the dogs as soon as he tracks down Chanel?" Priya asked.

"She's in hiding because he's a fucking dickwad shit," Tantum said. "We'll head there, and we'll switch cars. I have a whole network, and I know some cops. I'm not worried. The glaucoma bitches have got this. Awesome job turning into a bitch, by the way!" She ruffled Priya's hair, almost like she was patting her head.

"Did I look like a dog or a wolf?" Priya asked, not really caring.

"Something big and scary," Suzy said.

"Can you see when you're … whatever you are?" Priya couldn't think of a tactful way to put it.

"An oma," said Suzy, her voice partly muffled by a sweater she'd pulled over her head.

"A what?"

"An oma. Like a lipoma or an adenoma. A benign growth."

Tantum grinned. "Don't you get it yet? I told you right at the beginning. We're the glaucoma bitches. I'm the glauc—I've got the worst eyesight, but I'm small and black and reliable, almost invisible, like a Glock gun."

"You got your gun back?" Priya remembered to ask.

"Of course." Tantum showed off her leg holster. "Sure, a few bullets got embedded in his walls, but don't worry, I'll make sure this gun doesn't get traced back to us."

Priya sighed in relief, and her mind switched back to the puzzle. "So you're the glauc, or Glock. Suzy's the oma who can transform and move into interstitial spaces. And I'm the bitch."

"Got it in one! You're a smart cookie," said Tantum.

"Smart bitch in the kitch," said Suzy, riffing on the name of a once-popular series of books.

Priya laughed and howled with the canines and her glaucoma bitches as they zoomed onto the highway, reuniting the dogs with their mother.

MIND BENDER

BY ROWAN MARCI

CN: Gunshots, extortion, threats of harm/violence

Jada Antolini was not a villain. She was only tying this government clerk to a chair to help her parents out.

Her mom made a lap of the kitchen, stilettos clacking against the linoleum as she inspected the kitschy jar sets and fruit-patterned backsplash tiles. "Nice place. City pays you well?"

The clerk didn't answer. He had a rag stuffed in his mouth.

Her cousin held the official's arms tight while Jada whipped a cord into a handcuff knot around his wrists, blowing a strand of lavender hair out of her eyes. She should really be studying for her ninth grade history test. But her parents could never seem to do these jobs without her.

Straightening, she adjusted her cropped hoodie and glanced down at the clerk. He was shaking, a sheen of sweat coating his forehead. Jada felt kinda bad for the guy. Most of the people the Antolinis extorted were criminals, or were at least being paid off by criminals. But this dude seemed to run as straight as she'd ever seen, down to the smiling pictures of the wife and kid he was probably as faithful to as he was his job. The only things decorating Jada's apartment were bullet holes and newspaper clippings mentioning the Antolini family.

Her mom leaned back against the sink. "Listen, bub. We know there's a shipment of infusions coming in two weeks. A big one. We want *details*." Darla Antolini bared her teeth around the last word, lipstick red against the gleaming white.

But the government clerk just shook his head. Either he had no information, or he hadn't understood. The bulge of a hearing implant beneath his close-cropped hair suggested it might be the latter.

Jada rolled her eyes at her best friend, who was squashed against the wall between Jada's two hulking cousins, looking small, sharp-edged and unamused. Trinity smirked back, brushing aside her cloud of frizzy hair to finger her own implant. Jada's parents always refused to use sign language unless they absolutely had to.

Jada turned down the volume on her own implant just to spite them.

Her mom crossed the kitchen to lean into the clerk's face. "THE SHIPMENT! INFUSIONS! WHEN IS IT COMING?!" Her red lips stretched like a clown's.

"You have to unplug his mouth, doll." Jada's dad leaned against the fridge, hands tucked into the pockets of his imported Italian dress slacks. Giuseppe Antolini always dressed like an old-timey gangster in white collared button-downs with his black hair slicked back, taking the adage "dress for the job you want" very seriously.

Jada sighed. "The guy's got his volume down. He can't *hear* you, Ma."

Darla snatched the gag out of the official's mouth with one sharp fingernail. "Tell us when the shipment is coming." She hadn't acknowledged Jada, but at least she began to sign. Jada savored a moment of annoyance-tinged vindication.

"I want names," Darla went on. "Locations. Access points. Everything."

The clerk remained close-lipped. One of the cousins prodded at his head with the muzzle of a revolver.

Jada sighed, her dreams of seeing at least a "B" scrawled atop of tomorrow's history test evaporating. She'd paid attention in class, she knew about the global impact of the contagion that had torn through the human population thirty years ago, strange, and slippery, disguising itself as other diseases before researchers could figure out what was going on. Many who hadn't been deaf or hard-of-hearing became so after it, as well as many of the kids born since then. So, most people these days—excluding Darla and Giuseppe Antolini—used sign language along with speaking, since you could never really tell who was deaf and who wasn't.

But the change in the population's hearing status hadn't been the biggest one. Sure, that had affected the largest number of people. But some came out of that infection…different. Some people had been *changed*.

"I…I don't know anything other than the date," the clerk finally said. He had to speak aloud, since Jada had tied his hands behind the chair. "My clearance doesn't go higher than that."

MIND BENDER

Darla raised a penciled-on eyebrow. "That's not what our source at city hall tells us." When she straightened, Jada knew what was coming next. It would be her turn, or Trinity's. That was the price of having parents like Jada's, the price of being born with a genetic mutation that allowed her and Trinity to do things other people couldn't.

Trinity's hair twisting had progressed to full-on nail biting. She didn't like her role in the Antolinis' schemes any more than Jada did. But she played along, because Darla and Giuseppe's criminal enterprise was the only thing standing between her dad and the powerful crime bosses he'd betrayed.

As for Jada…

Jada's mom locked eyes with her. "Sweetie?" she crooned.

Jada cocked her head with an exaggerated squint. "What?" she signed, gesturing to her ear. "Can't hear you."

Darla's lips pressed thin. She could have signed back, angry red nails flashing. Instead, she marched around the clerk's chair, fingers gouging Jada's arm as she dragged her around to face him.

The guy's eyes were bloodshot and scared. He must have known there was only one reason you brought a fourteen-year-old along on a job like this.

"Sorry," Jada signed. Then she took a deep breath, cupped her hands, and twisted.

The clerk yelped, lurching backward in his chair.

"Again!" Darla shrieked.

Jada grimaced, shifting her hands back and forth with less force than she could have. The clerk moaned anyway, swaying hard enough to topple his chair if someone wasn't holding it steady.

The guy didn't deserve this, really, he didn't.

"You can do better than that," Jada's dad murmured from the fridge.

This was the reason her parents paraded her around at parties, let her roam Antolini-controlled streets like some feral princess. She was a Mind Bender. Her mutation allowed her to sense another person's consciousness—not see it, but *feel* it—and forge a connection she could manipulate with a flick of her fingers. She could make the world as they saw it change, make left become right, big become small, make space from their viewpoint expand, shatter, flip upside down.

And she was good at it.

"How does it feel?" Darla's eyes gleamed as she leaned over the clerk's shoulder. For a moment, Jada considered bending the mind of the guy holding the chair so the whole thing would topple backward onto her mom. Seeing Darla's cheetah-print butt hit the floor was a hard opportunity to pass up.

But the guy holding the chair was Trinity's dad, and Jada liked him, all six-foot-three and two hundred fifty pounds of him. Leo had carried her on his shoulders enough times to make Trinity jealous, bought her empanadas down the block when her parents hadn't bothered to feed her. Plus, Leo had been trained to resist Mind Benders.

"Stop!" the clerk gasped. Jada stilled her hands, but the man retched anyway. "I don't know anything! I swear!"

He could be telling the truth. From what Jada had overheard, this dude just handled data and scheduling at the government office downtown. But any chance the Antolinis had to get their hands on illegal infusions—the real deal, the big money—they would take. "Is that so?" Darla pursed her lips at the clerk. "Maybe this will help jog your memory. Trinity?"

Jada saw cold resolve in her best friend's eyes as she straightened from her spot on the wall.

Jada didn't want to watch. She turned to examine the clerk's family photos instead, wondering if motion sickness was contagious, because this dude looked like a good guy and her own stomach was churning. He looked like the type who'd let his kid do constructive things with their mutation, things like putting out fires and rescuing old ladies from oncoming trains. Guys like him would definitely send their kids to Peacemakers Academy.

Last week in history class, they'd learned about the three choices that had emerged after the virus changed people. In those days, new mutants had been leveling buildings and taking out entire neighborhoods with their powers. There were three options now to manage mutations like Jada's and Trinity's, three alternatives to destroying yourself and everything else within a three-block radius.

Government suppressants were one. It was the choice incentives and ad campaigns wanted you to want.

Infusions were another, a method the government had been quick to outlaw. Infusions focused a mutant's power like a refraction lens on a laser. The government's official stance was that infusions were untested, unsafe. But everyone knew the real reason. They feared mutants' power.

Choice number three was Peacemakers Academy. Some rich do-gooder had founded the school for the sole purpose of public protection, no agenda other than preparing mutants to keep the city safe.

As a representative of the criminal underworld who'd been using illegal infusions since birth, Jada had to pretend to hate the Academy. Really, she wanted to be there. She and Trinity had spent more time than she cared to admit hanging off the school's wrought-iron fence, staring up at the massive old brownstones with filched lollipops between their teeth. They'd launched insults at the clean, uniformed students crossing the lawns, knowing full well their knock-off street fashion and juvenile delinquency placed them firmly on the other side of the gate.

But at night, when Trinity was at her own apartment and Darla and Giuseppe schemed downstairs, Jada lay in bed imagining that the clothes she'd laid out for the next school day were actually a Peacemakers Academy uniform.

A different identity. A different life.

She'd never shared that private dream with her best friend. She wondered what Trinity would think as her friend crossed the clerk's kitchen with a raised chin and hard eyes. But before Trinity could lift her hands, her head snapped toward the living room. Everyone else's eyes followed. Jada peered around a cousin, turning up her hearing implant's volume just in time to catch the *snick* of the apartment door.

"Well, well, well." Darla Antolini grinned as she paced to the doorway. "Looks like elementary school's out for the day."

A tiny kid stood just inside the living room. She couldn't have been more than six or seven, a pixie with skinny brown limbs and twin ponytails tied up with pompoms, a flower-print backpack sliding off her shoulder. Her mouth hung open.

"Mavis!" the clerk cried. "Run!"

"Daddy!" screamed the little girl. She took a step toward the kitchen then stopped, eyes darting from face to face.

"Come on, sweetie," Darla beckoned, expression more smirk than smile. "Come meet Daddy's new friends."

Jada's heart beat hard enough to ramp up the ringing in her ears to a roar.

"Run, Mavis!" The clerk's voice was hoarse with effort. "Daddy's okay, but I need you to *run*."

The little girl stayed frozen—breath fast and shallow—but her gaze flicked to Jada and stayed there.

"Come see Daddy." Darla took a step into the living room and extended her hand. The kid jerked away, dropping her backpack and whirling toward the door.

"Leo!" Darla barked.

Trinity's dad crossed the living room in two heavy strides and scooped the kid up by the waist. The little girl kicked and wailed as he carried her into the kitchen. He was gentle with her, the same way he'd always been with Trinity, yet she looked small and breakable in his hands.

"No!" the clerk moaned. The cord Jada had tied rubbed his wrists raw. "Please—"

Darla shuffle-stepped to the kid and pinched her chin. "Adorable!" she signed, smile as sharp as her nails. "It'd be a shame if something happened to her, wouldn't it?"

The back of Jada's throat turned sour. This was a kid. A little *kid*. They'd been shaking down schemers, dealers, and crooks for years, but threatening an innocent kid was a whole new level of messed up.

"Please!" the clerk wailed. "Let her go! I'll do anything, I swear!"

"Talk, then." Darla didn't bother signing, but her lips were easy enough to read.

Jada exchanged a glance with her friend. Trinity's eyes had gone wide.

The clerk sobbed. "I don't know anything else! I told you!"

Darla stepped back. "Trinity?"

It was just a word, just a name. But the sound echoed over and over in Jada's head.

Darla Antolini wasn't much of a mom, or a crime boss for that matter. But for the last eight years, her influence had been the only thing keeping Trinity and Leo safe from the enemies they'd made. This was the reason, Jada told herself, that Trinity began to inch forward.

"Mavis!" the clerk cried. It took two cousins to hold his chair down.

Darla yanked the kid's hand up and squashed every finger but her pinky into a fist. "Let's start here, shall we?"

Jada's skin crawled. Somewhere, her parents had inched over a line, and she hadn't even noticed. They'd gone past counterculture sentiments and "doing what it takes to survive," past opportunism, power grabs and plain old greed. Somewhere along the way they'd edged past ruthlessness into cruelty, and Jada had been fast asleep.

Until now.

Everything in the kitchen seemed sharper, brighter. The overhead lights, the discordant squeal of chair legs on linoleum. Her mother's sneer, teeth gleaming white. Leo's jaw ticking as Trinity raised a trembling hand. The kid's muffled whimper as a reluctant flame sparked to life, inches from her pinky finger.

"NO!" the clerk screamed.

Jada's hands shot up. Maybe it was instinct. Maybe it was the part of her that wasn't Giuseppe and Darla Antolini's daughter, the part of her that secretly longed to be a student at Peacemakers Academy. But she *was* Darla and Giuseppe's kid, and she knew exactly what this was going to cost her.

She wouldn't be able to come back from this.

Jada swept her palms outward. For everyone except Trinity and the little girl, the kitchen exploded.

Her cousins yelped and stumbled. Her mom shrieked and her dad dropped to a knee. Leo stayed on his feet, but his hands fell away from the kid's shoulders.

Jada dodged between the cousins and skirted around her parents. Grabbing Trinity's wrist, she held out a hand to the little girl. "Let's go."

She wasn't sure why the kid listened. Jada may not have been a villain, but she wasn't exactly good, either. But the little girl blinked at her with wide brown eyes and took her hand.

Jada bolted into the living room, pulling Trinity and the kid after her. "Go!" she ordered, pushing them toward the door. She whirled around just in time to see the cousins raising revolvers.

Jada threw her hands down, making the floor collapse beneath them in their minds. She didn't wait to see who lost their balance and fell; she yanked the door open and bolted down the stairs after her friend.

"Go, go, go!" Their footsteps were thunderous, drowning out the sound of what was happening behind her. Jada overtook the kid on the second floor landing, scooping her up to run faster. Her breath was so loud, she would have missed the shot completely if cinderblock debris hadn't sprayed her in the face.

Jada spun, shoving the kid behind her. From the third floor landing, a cousin leveled a silenced revolver at her. She had just enough time to throw a hand out and twist, making his world spin and his unbalanced body tumble down the stairs. Then Leo vaulted over her cousin's knocked-out form and grabbed her wrists in one meaty hand.

Jada's breath whooshed out as he yanked her around, shielding her from view of the staircase. "What're you doing, kid?" he hissed, his free hand trembling as he signed, "Do you know how much danger you're putting us in?"

Jada winced, glancing at Trinity. She hadn't meant to jeopardize their safety. She was only trying to help the kid, save Trinity from becoming what neither of them wanted to be.

"Knock it off, Dad," Trinity mumbled. But she shrank under Leo's glower.

"You wanna see what happens if you run away?" he ground out. "Where you gonna go, Tee? We ain't got nobody left. And I can't protect you if I'm dead."

Trinity's gaze hit the floor, along with Jada's heart.

"That goes for you, too." Leo turned his scorching gaze on her. "Where you think you're gonna be safe in this town?"

He was right. The Antolinis may not be the most powerful crime family, but in their corner of the city, they were kings. In these neighborhoods, Jada wasn't just somebody. She was untouchable.

And if she left? She had nothing, she had no one.

But there was one place she might be safe. Maybe.

"Let me go, Leo." She shoved against his vice-like grip. "Let me get the kid out. You'd want the same if it was Trinity."

Leo's eyes softened. Jada knew that everything he did, all the people he'd roughed up for her parents, had been to keep his daughter safe.

"Be quick about it then." He dropped her wrists, narrowing his eyes. "And come right back. Do whatever you gotta do to get back in."

Jada clenched her teeth. She wasn't coming back, and she certainly wasn't going to kiss Darla and Giuseppe's behinds. But she gave Leo a stiff nod, and that seemed to satisfy him.

Trinity was another story. She and Jada had been inseparable since the age of six when Leo had stumbled into Antolini territory with his daughter in his arms. But now Trinity's eyes were cold, remote, and Jada couldn't see herself in them anymore.

"You coming, Tee?"

Trinity blinked. "You go. I should stay here and help clean up this mess."

Jada didn't think pleading would do any good. And cussing would just piss her off. So, she walled up her heart until she couldn't feel the pain any more. She'd gotten used to it, with her parents.

"See you, then," she said.

"See you." Trinity's fingers were limp as she signed.

Jada's gaze didn't linger on their faces. She didn't look back as she ran, ran with the kid until her lungs were burning, until the kid couldn't keep up and Jada had to carry her again. She ran without hearing anything but the breath in her lungs and the beating of her heart, not knowing if anyone was following her. She ran as if someone was, as if she could escape herself and all she had done if she just went fast enough.

She ran until they reached an alley by the subway station, where sketchy restaurants shouldered up to finance brokerages and government-run pharmacies. Jada slumped down against a wall and the little girl puddled in her lap, clinging to her hoodie. Not only did she look like a pixie, she weighed about as much. "Mavis, right?" Jada signed.

The girl nodded.

"You got somewhere to go?"

The kid bit her lip. "My grandma's." Her fingers were small, clean, like someone who loved her had taught her to wash them before every meal. Jada couldn't believe her mom wanted to burn one of them.

"Good." Jada swiped a sweaty lock of hair out of her eyes. "Go on, then. Go straight to your grandma's and don't stop until you get there."

The kid didn't budge. "But my dad…"

"He'll be all right. I promise." Trinity and Leo would make sure the clerk spilled everything he knew. Then her parents would leave him. The last thing the Antolinis wanted was a dead government official getting the Peacemakers on their backs.

The girl's lip quivered.

"Oh, stop it." Jada pushed the kid off her lap. "I told you he'd be okay, and I meant it. Now get to your grandma's before I make the world fall over on you."

It wasn't the nicest thing to say. The kid probably should have been scared, or at least pissed. But she gave Jada a gap-toothed smile before scurrying off.

Jada watched her pom-pom ponytails bob down the stairs of the subway terminal. Then she stood and brushed off her cargo pants.

MIND BENDER

Past the Antolinis' territory and the business district, past the park and the neighborhood school, a wrought iron fence separated sprawling brownstones and acres of green lawn from the rest of the city. Jada knew the way by heart.

Only rich kids got accepted into Peacemakers Academy, everyone knew that. But a wealthy philanthropist had founded the place, so there had to be some sort of scholarship program. They had to at least offer sanctuary to people who needed it. Wasn't doing good deeds their whole deal?

Jada would convince them to let her in. She wasn't a villain, after all, though she wasn't exactly good either. But maybe—some day—she could learn to be.

MUTANT PRIDE

BY SHANNON BARNSLEY

CN: Medical neglect, ableism, disabled people being used as props for promotional/political purposes, boarding school uniform inspection, mention of a pandemic, teleporting into a locker room (for platonic purposes), toxic positivity

"This training is gonna kill me." I rubbed my subluxed shoulder, sitting down on the bench. The barometric pressure wasn't bad today, but my joints were already protesting.

Mel set down her Hydroflask and came to sit beside me, lacing her fingers into mine and rhythmically rubbing my palm with her thumb. The sigils on her arms, their normal black ink less apparent against her dravite umber complexion, began to glow, gold as her nail polish. She whispered in Archaic Latin or maybe Phoenicio-Punic. I could never keep them all straight, barely managing a C in Intro to Ancient Languages of the Mediterranean. Either way,

I could already feel the effect on my pulse and circulation as the tachycardia and brain fog began to abate.

"You're a lifesaver, Mel. I owe you one."

Her eyes went bloodshot and her irises shone gold before settling back to her usual deep brown. "Lemme borrow your notes for the geology exam, we'll call it even."

"Knock, knock." Hallie Hayes, a junior like me, appeared just past our row of lockers, the air shimmering around her like a heat mirage.

"No teleporting allowed in the locker room, Hallie," Mel chided as she pulled off the jacket of the standard-issue field uniform we all wore for our training regimen, be it parkour, cardio, strength-training, mixed martial arts, battle simulation, what-have-you.

"It's the girls' locker room. I'm a girl." Hallie looked around, noting that we were the only ones in here, everyone else in the showers or gone by now. She flicked back her cranberry-mauve braid, the vibrant hue a sharp contrast with her alabaster skin. "Anyway, Rico and Miski had to go into the city to stop Persona-Non-Grotto from unleashing a kraken in the Hudson; Reyhan, Kaz, and Peyton are still trapped in 1872; and Alternate-Timeline-Reyhan is eloping with Rico's clone, so Dr. Mews needs you two to tap in today."

"Today?" I asked. "What's today?"

"Honestly, do you even read the calendar?" Hallie asked. "Do you know how hard Anonymiss works trying to keep it updated with battles on any number of continents, dimensions, or galaxies at the drop of a hat? She syncs everything across time zones, temporal anomalies, and temporal shifts and you can't even look at the damn thing?"

"Spit it out, Hallie." Mel took her shower caddy out of her locker.

"Poppy Pattou. *Perk Up with Poppy*," Hallie said. "Merman's been roped in too, but he can't really give tours, what with the gills and all, and the camera crew doesn't have a waterproof mic to put on him. Besides, they want more young faces to keep the focus on Mewseum Preparatory as a school for, y'know, differently abled kids rather than-"

"A paramilitary training cell for vigilantes?" Mel finished.

"Yeah, that. Optics, you get it."

"You can just say mutants," I said, unzipping my own jacket, which bore Dr. Mews' signature µ symbol on the chest. "It's on half the merch anyway." I opened my locker and whipped out my keycard with its 'Mutant Pride' lanyard. "I mean, sure, I can shapeshift into any animal in the order Carnivora and not everyone can do that, but not everyone can sing Italian aria or shoot an English longbow, so, if you mean mutant, say mutant."

"Well, we have a few non-mutant enhanced individuals at the school and one extraterrestrial exchange student, so it's more all-encompassing," Hallie explained.

"Burs'ukh says Martians don't like the term either," I said. "Defining Martians by what's typical for Earthlings is kind of presumptuous."

"Fine," conceded Hallie. "Enhanced individuals then. Happy now?"

"I wouldn't search that with the safety off," said Mel with a laugh. "Just say mutant. It's not gonna banish us back to the fifth dimension or summon some eldritch being if you speak it aloud."

"Anyway," said Hallie, "Mews needs you in the conservatory in an hour. Wear your school uniforms, not your costumes. And shower. Please. You smell like a wet dog."

"Well, I was a collie a quarter of an hour ago, so…"

My words faded as Hallie did, the glimmer in the air lingering where she'd just been.

"There goes my extra time in the archaeoastronomy wing," Mel sighed. "Hope we finish before biochem. I'm so behind."

"You're a literal blood mage, you'll be fine. Besides, you know Liam would love to tutor you."

"Hush." Mel did a shushing dog hand command. "Down, girl. Liam and I are just friends."

"Yes, Miski caught you being such *good friends* in the herbarium last semester," I teased, grabbing my own shower bag.

"You know how much I like poisonous plants," she said. "Now c'mon. Mews will kill us if we ruin her big TV spot."

■ ▪ ■ ▪ ■ ▪ ▪ ■ ▪ ▪ ▪ ▪ ▪ ▪ ▪ ▪ ▪ ■ ■

An hour later Mel and I were standing in the conservatory, the smell of old leather and lacquered wood heavy in my nose. My senses always took a while to dim back to human levels after a shift.

Beside us, Archie was perched like a parrot eagerly awaiting some shiny new toy. His wheelchair was uncharacteristically civilian today, adorned only with the pocket safeguarding his pencils and blueprints—not to mention snacks. Usually, it was tricked out with some modification or other, be it all-terrain treads, rocket blasters, or whatever the occasion (or the whims of an exuberant twelve-year-old techie) might require.

Professor Bhattacharya inspected the three of us like a drill sergeant. She frowned at the safety pins in Mel's skirt and blazer and the sigils drawn in white-out on her ripped tights, not to mention Archie's sandy brown curls that defied all attempts to keep them flat over his tan, freckled forehead. I hovered warily near Archie, his Fishercat t-shirt visible under his own blazer. Promotional materials loved Archie—and, yeah, everybody loved Archie, as they should—, but the kind of gaze media types always fixed on him got my hackles up. The same way my skin crawled when Dr. Mews called us students her "little superheroes".

"They're finishing up with Dr. Mews now," said Professor Bhattacharya.

We'd heard the story a million times. Any student here could recite it by heart. How one Dr. Carolyn Mews had been on a dig in '78—an Etruscan tomb in Caisra—when one of the archaeology students unwittingly opened an ancient phial, releasing a mystical virus. The strange pathogen was global within a fortnight, with people around the world suffering unexplained fevers, chills, and other immune responses. Then, just as fast, it was gone. It might have faded from the public consciousness altogether, just some odd blip on the radar lost between the Nuclear Non-Proliferation Act and the death of John Lennon.

Then, while recovering in Firenze, Dr. Mews, patient zero of the μ-virus, as it would come to be known, discovered she could suddenly and inexplicably read the Etruscan language. And the Harappan language. Any written language, no matter how unknown an isolate or indecipherable the writing system. An omniglot, they called her. A mutant—the first of many.

MUTANT PRIDE

As the world soon realized, something about the virus mutated cells in certain people, awakening new powers. Pyrokinesis. Astral projection. Regeneration. Mutants were cropping up in every country on every continent and the world was utterly unprepared for the complete paradigm shift they found themselves in the middle of. Laws, social attitudes, and consensual reality spun out, trying to keep pace with unprecedented change, the likes of which no human society had ever seen.

Politicians like Congressman Irving made it their life's work to cordon or excise us while others sought to pressgang us into service as special ops or pet superheroes. Scientists, meanwhile, tried to cure, replicate, or use us. Dr. Cavan Wright, an archeo-engineer on the dig with Dr. Mews, armed with the ability to raise any number of creatures from the deep, had gone on the offensive for mutant liberation, becoming public enemy number one and taking the name Persona-Non-Grotto.

A septuagenarian now, he was apparently still not content to exit stage left and retire the supervillain game. But, then again, Dr. Mews was also still offering education and shelter to at-risk mutant youth by day and operating world-famous superhero team, Dr. μ and the μ-tants, by night. Dr. μ was rarely in the field herself anymore, but she operated from the command center while someone else, usually Influencer these days, relayed her orders on the ground.

Few remained of the original team. Only Dr. μ and Burningman were still active superheroes, everyone else from their generation— we think, we honestly have no idea how old Burningman is—having died or faded into obscurity by now. But new heroes were always popping up to fill in the ranks, be it in the field or the public eye. Inaya Bhattacharya, better known as HERicane, and Brett Sanders, a.k.a. Influencer, were the golden geese of the moment as Bob "Fishercat" Fischer, a grizzled, battle-weary fan favorite, slowly sundowned.

Burningman was the eternal alternate, always just off stage, in the back of the group in every photo through the years. We knew almost nothing about him. Nobody knew where he'd come from before the virus. He had that ambiguous look that could be from almost anywhere. Iranian maybe? Italian? South Asian? Latino?

"If you're showing off your powers today, Professor, could you go easy?" I asked HERicane. "My bones are already killing me."

Just then Poppy Pattou swooped into the room like the world's peppiest carrion bird, a cameraman and boom mic guy following after her. Influencer, Dr. Mews, Burningman, and Fishercat trailed behind them, their own interviews concluded. Fishercat didn't interview well these days, but he was always up for striking a few poses and throwing out a catchphrase or two, which usually went over like a piñata bursting at a child's birthday party.

After oozing friendliness all over Professor Bhattacharya, Poppy turned on me, the oldest of our band of Little-Mutant-Annies. Dr. Mews stepped forward to introduce us, but Poppy shut her down, saying she wanted to catch more informal, candid footage. Poppy, who must have been a damn general in a form fitting floral print dress if she could overpower Dr. Mews so effectively, returned her attention to me.

"Poppy Pattou," she said, shaking my hand off. "It's Haze, right?"

"Um, Haze is the teleporter," I said. "I'm Mist."

"Oh, the shifter, of course," she said. "Noelani Peltierre. Sixteen. Originally from Pearl City. Saved a bus full of tourists last week."

"Yep… that's me…" I was suddenly very aware of my hair being behind my ears. I tried to push one side forward without it looking too intentional, my cheeks hot.

"You'll give us a demonstration, right?" Poppy asked, enthused.

I glanced at the faculty present. "I told Dr. Mews. I don't do demonstrations anymore."

"Oh, come on," said Poppy, "it's for the school. Very humanizing to see you all in your element doing your thing…"

"I have Ehlers-Danlos Syndrome," I said firmly. "My joints have a hard enough time staying in place without me rearranging my skeleton for parlor tricks."

Poppy looked at me. "Was that a result of the μ-virus?"

"No, it ran in the family before that," I told her. "I mean, technically] it's a mutation, but… not that kind."

"Oh," said Poppy disappointedly. She turned to the cameraman. "Gabe, you can go ahead and cut that. Our viewership isn't interested in pre-existing conditions."

"Hi. Yeah. Standing right here." My blazer suddenly felt like a furnace.

Dr. Mews shot me a warning look.

"Nightingale," said Mel forcefully beside me, sticking her hand out to shake. "Known around here as Mel Philliskirk. I'm fifteen; I come from Telluride; and, no, I did not do the tattoos myself, nor can I recommend a tattoo artist. They appeared on my body when my powers manifested. I'm a blood mage, but I know that term doesn't play well in the Central Time Zone, so you can call me a hemokenetic. Basically, if blood does it or has it, I can affect it."

"I've not heard that one before," said Poppy. "Hemokenetic. I like it. And I love your nail polish!"

"Tut's Tomb Gold. I can get you the link." Mel explained, "I'm really the healer of the party, but my power can be offensive in a pinch. Bit brutal, though. Anyway, I know Archie is dying to give you a demonstration."

Archie was scrabbling for his blueprints like a scientist in a disaster movie trying to show the brass his calculations before the asteroid/aliens/irradiated lizard zombies struck.

"You're the- what was it called again?" Poppy asked. "I'm sorry, my notes were all for Rico, Peyton, and Kazimir, so I'm flying by the seat of my pants here."

"A technograph." Archie beamed. "If I have the blueprints for something and I alter them, that thing alters in real time, so… whatever I can draw, I can make it real. My course load is mostly engineering, architecture, and art classes. The better I get at them, the more I can do."

"That's awesome!" said Poppy. "Now, can you tell us your name?"

"Oh, yeah, I'm Archie. Archie Kurtzberg Torres. Archi-tech." He straightened his blueprints into an orderly stack. "I was born in Curitiba, but I've been at Mewseum Preparatory since I was eight."

"I know you and Influencer do a lot of ambassadorial work," said Poppy.

"Oh, yes," said Brett, cutting in with his flouncy golden hair and smarmy golden boy smile. "We at Mewseum Preparatory really try to engage with the global community to better their understanding of mutants *and µ-tants*…"

He gave a little wink at the camera that made me roll my eyes. Mel's pointed nail bit into my arm. It didn't take a telepath to get the message: pokerface. Even if Brett was literally the worst. Sure, he could fly and manipulate endorphins via touch, but his only qualification for leadership was his jawline, and his idea of student counseling/team cohesion began and ended with "Vibe check?"

"… make the world a more secure, more inclusive place." There was that dental-advert-whitemy-dad-is-running-for-somethingso-this-Christmas-card-was-staged-I-don't-even-know-how-to-ski smile again. "We also love visiting the local hospitals when we get a chance. It really helps the kids to feel braver when they can meet their heroes. But, of course, they're the real heroes."

I contemplated throwing myself from the stained-glass window beyond the bookshelves. We were on the second story. If I shifted into a cat, I could probably make it unscathed. It would be murder on my joints, but my pain level was already at negligent homicide, courtesy of the barometric pressure, so might as well go for broke. Either I'd misread the meteorology report, Weathervania was on the attack again, or HERicane had not taken my request to heart.

"I do wonder why I'm not invited on more of those hospital trips," said Mel. She flourished her hands. "I mean, I can't heal them, but I can give them a white blood cell boost or a little extra plasma."

I looked at Mel, as did everyone else. She'd never gone rogue in public before.

"Oh, um," Brett began, "yeah, scheduling conflicts always seem to… But I'm a tactile opiokenetic. Who doesn't need an endorphin rush? A couple high fives and those kiddos are ready to take on anything."

"Y'know, if I recall correctly, the one time I was invited, Archie couldn't go because the building wasn't accessible," Mel said. "Which makes no sense; it's a medical facility. Who the hell makes a medical facility inaccessible?"

"Your power must be really helpful for that," said Poppy, honing back in on Archie. "If something's inaccessible, you can just go down to city hall and get the blueprints. Amazing."

"Actually, I can't." Archie's face fell and his shoulders shrank. "City hall… isn't accessible…"

"Are you serious?!" It burst out before I could stop myself. Yep, definitely tucking and rolling out the window.

"Miss Peltierre," said Dr. Mews in her headmaster voice.

"Dr. Mews," I replied, pushing my straight black hair back out of my eyes and meeting her glare.

"Gabe, Gabe, stay on her," Poppy hissed.

"If you want a story, Poppy, how 'bout the rampant medical neglect among the μ-tants," I said. "We encounter unknown pathogens on alien planets; untested, jerry-rigged technology; radiation in space; serums with no FDA approval or even human trials; whatever the hell time dilations and phase shifting do to the human body, and who knows what else? Do you know how widespread concussions are at Mewseum Prep? It's like the NFL up in here. Fishercat's been dropkicked off more buildings than anyone without a regeneration power should be able to walk away from. I mean, yeah, he has super strength, but he's not invulnerable. Plus, I don't think it plays well with his other power."

"The kid's right," came Fishercat's gravelly voice, his scarred brow furrowing. "When I get someone else's memories, mine get a little scrambled. Plus, every time the timelines change or the multiverses converge, I'm lost for weeks."

"Fischer," said Dr. Mews, looking cornered. "Come now. We've known each other for decades. Why didn't you say anything? If there's something you need-"

"He needs a neuropsychological work-up like yesterday," I said. "You keep sending him off to find himself when all he ever finds is a bar fight and another government conspiracy."

"Irving is a real piece o' work," Fishercat growled. "But, yeah. That executive functioning workbook Inaya gave me isn't enough. I need executive functioning to remember the workbook. It's a problem."

"Fischer, let's talk about this in my office after-"

"Like we talked after I found my long-lost brother, Lynx? Don't count on it, pal," said Fishercat. "I have a real problem. I was trying to get some clam chowder at the mess hall last week, but I couldn't remember the words 'clam' or 'chowder', so I was left standing there—next to Wellerman, for the record—trying to figure out how to ask for Ariel's bra soup without making the dozen rugrats behind me all titter or twitter or whatever. I need to see a real doctor. Or you need to bring me a real doctor so I can bite them and remember going to med school."

"It really is amazing how you can acquire memories via bite," said Poppy. "Do you know how that works?"

"Lady, I don't know how a damn thing in this place works," he snapped. "I tried to change the thermostat once and ended up swapping the polarities of an entire miniaturized planet kept in a terr- terrari- one of those little plant snowglobes in the xenobotany classroom. Another time, I tried to talk to Wellerman, Merman, and Burningman about organizing a shanty night—rhythmic motion, music, and social synchronization help with PTSD. We have plenty of that at this school... Where was I?"

"Shanties," Archie said.

"Right," said Fishercat. "Anyway, turned out Wellerman was mindjacked by the Hitchhiker after a near death experience; Merman was a mirrorverse doppelgänger who'd stashed our Merman in the Poconos; and Burningman was, well, Burningman, but then he went full phoenix and burst into flames again."

"I do that," said Burningman apologetically in his obscure accent no one had ever been able to place. "That's why I haven't aged since… well… y'know, nevermind."

"Since 1978, right?" HERicane narrowed her eyes suspiciously. "Sure, Inaya, let's go with that."

"Gabe, this is incredible," whispered Poppy. "We're getting off the morning show for sure. Next stop: primetime, hard-hitting news."

"God damn it, HERicane, stop messing with the barometric pressure!" I shouted. Forget negligent homicide, my joint pain was at manslaughter, at least.

"Sorry," she said. "It's tied to my mental focus, and I have no idea what's happening right now."

It was at that moment that Fishercat rushed Burningman, picking him up in a full nelson. Burningman tried to barbecue Fishercat, but Mel came to his aid, eyes blazing gold, the whites gone completely red. Fire needs oxygen. Oxygen is carried in the blood. Fishercat sank his suddenly apparent fangs into the now-blue-faced Burningman's duster-clad shoulder, his own eyes glazing over as memories flashed before him.

"My god…" Fishercat stumbled back in awe as Burningman crumpled to the floor. "He's not a mutant, he's an immortal Etruscan undertaker. He left the phial. He funded Dr. Mews's dig!"

"Not cool, Fischer," Burningman said, gasping for breath as Mel loosed her hold. Though rapidly returning to normal, his face was still tinged a bloodless blue lank hair in disarray. "And... I'm a... tomb priest. Not... an undertaker."

"I'm Poppy Pattou and I'm gonna win a Pullitzer," Poppy whispered ecstatically into the camera.

"Lemme at 'im!" My shoulder cracked audibly as I jumped the camera, rounding on Burningman. "You're paying my damn physical therapy bill, you brimstone reaper."

INVISIBLE DEE

BY E.D.E. BELL

CN: Ableism, invisible disability, mentions of fire and policing

"**B**ut I can see you."

Superheroes didn't get to pick their own names. And so, Invisible Dee was used to giving a tightly polite smile when people learned she had no powers of literal invisibility. No cloak. No dust. No dimensional shift.

"And you *are* disabled?" The check-in volunteer asked it politely, in a way Dee knew was meant to protect the community. Despite that she'd registered for MightyCon, a gathering specific to disabled superheroes.

"Yes," she answered, and, check-in completed, nervously went to hover near one of the plain, segmented walls that had been slid out to enclose the Opening Ceremony room.

"Please, have a seat," another volunteer said, looking harried. "Oh, I'm fine."

The volunteer did not seem pleased, but Dee was hoping there might be someone here she knew, and wanted to wait to see if they might sit with her. Which, in itself, added worry in case she waited too long, and missed the chance to sit with someone in whom she found comfort. Especially if they were more popular.

Of course, that assumed someone she knew might be here. "I work during the day," several people had reminded her. Perhaps, then, she needed a plan, in case. Dee liked to meet new people, but sitting so close in with a whole table of them would be difficult.

Several tables had a few widely spaced chairs. *Reserved for mobility device users*, a sign made clear.

She glanced over at a table near the back. It was by the kitchen, and the door behind would prevent her from relaxing and cause her to jump, but perhaps that table would be less crowded. She could sit there, and maybe move a couple of the chairs toward the wall.

The kitchen was another worry. She'd submitted her diet, but it had been listed on her registration under "preferences" and not "needs". Eating was not a preference, and without food she'd grow light-headed. There was a snack in her bag, but then they'd think her rude.

Dee glanced at a noise to see the front doors being closed. "We need you to take your seat," a friendly voice said, ushering her toward a table of loud laughter and capes and masks.

With a breath, she sat.

The table was crowded, and she tried not to let her eyes fix on any one person, while somehow trying to smile at them all. Her tablemates became a blur of red latex and flashy logos, a bright yellow headwrap, a jeweled head brace, and the silvery shine of a custom bottle. Dee's comfortable black ensemble suddenly felt plain. She looked down, for a safer place to rest her eyes. Someone tapped around a small screen with a pinky finger, while another seemed to be adjusting their height and angle against the white-draped table.

"Invisible Dee," someone read from her nametag. "She, or any pronouns."

Dee looked back up. It was a hero in a shimmery purple corset, with a plunging purple neckline.

In the next seat, the hero in red smiled. "Then, she must not be invisible now. Unless she is a hovering nametag."

"Are you here with one of the attendees?" the first hero asked.

"Oh, no, I'm here for the conference," Dee answered. "I'm mentally disabled," she followed, twinging at the nearly-automatic addendum. For a moment, Dee worried they were going to ask—that she'd have to go through it all again. But just then, a server came by with a warm, inviting loaf of bread.

"Excuse me," Dee asked, adding, as quietly as she could, a question about the ingredients.

"It's bread," the server said with a shrug. "We have gluten-free bread if you need that."

"No thank you," Dee responded, eager to move on from the peering faces around the table. She picked up her water.

A booming sound from the front of the room made her jump, give a little scream, and spill the water, which ran out, into the bread. Dee looked up to see a burst of an obscuring substance, like a cloud, had somehow exploded near the front entrance. Security rushed from their corners of the room, but in the clearing of fog, where

Dee expected to see a hovering figure peering down villainously, there was none.

A voice boomed out. "Not too disabled to have a convention?" The doors burst open, and a person leapt through them, accompanied by a whipping sound as she flipped once high in the air, landing on her feet, atop the low conference stage.

Dee's heart flared. Not only was this the same abuse these heroes were here to escape, she thought with pain of the heroes who had not been able to join in person, and those for whom virtual had not been possible either.

It had been too hard for too long, and this *villain* had the nerve to—

"Meet Bootstrap Betty. 'Why is she here?'" The villain, slender within a tightly belted off-white bodysuit, cackled excitedly. "I'm here to close down this party so you can get back to *work*."

What looked like two leather whips flung out from her huge, spiked boots, and before Dee could realize what she intended, Betty snapped them through the air and around the banquet hall chandelier, which broke from its mounting. As the mix of lightbulbs and plastic crystals crashed down and plummeted the room into darkness, the hero in red flew upward, and Dee heard a whirring noise in the darkness and screams from the center of the room. Terrified, she opened her eyes to realize emergency lighting had turned on, and that the chandelier's pieces had been shrunken mid-air, so that only a tiny mess of glinting glass and tiny sparkles lay crashed on the center table.

In a hurry, people stood, wheeled, or otherwise readied, glancing around in fierce solidarity. Betty raised her whips.

"Betty! You too?" Dee laughed as she walked toward the front of the room, a sudden boldness overtaking her.

"Who are you?" Betty asked, her fingers tightening around the whips.

"Invisible Dee."

Betty relaxed a bit. "Well, that explains how you got in." She glanced around at the room. "Looks like they're going to try and fight back; could use the assist." "Funny, that's all we want too." Betty snapped her head over.

"I told you. I'm invisible. They never see me coming." Dee held up her dagger in one shaking hand and clutched the pair of straps she'd just severed in other, standing, steadfast. The straps in her hands wriggled, strengthening to reattach to Betty's boots.

Well, she couldn't be a superhero without a tiny monologue. And no way was she letting these straps go back to being used against anyone here. She posed a bit. "Oh, and I'm stubborn as all *fuck*."

Betty, clearly stalling for a plan, laughed in a forced nonchalance. "So that's your superpower, then? Being determinably unremarkable?"

Now Dee giggled. "Nope! My superpower is that my heart is made of *fire*." Raising the bootstraps into the air, her chest lit up, and glowed through her unzipped hoodie, and the straps from Betty's boots lit into supermagic flame, incinerating into a stinky little pile of ash that Dee walked right over in her old, worn, fuzzyshoes.

Feeling too shaky now to do much more, she wobbled in place. Behind her, she heard a rush. An arm steadied her and pulled her back into a seat.

And with the spin of an electric wheelchair, a web wound itself like a cage around Betty, who hovered within it, floating, her arms flailing helplessly.

Around her, the staff and guests were gathering, assisting the heroes in putting the room back into shape. A kind face appeared before Dee. "How can I help?"

"I need some time and a little space. And can you call one of my friends? I could use a hug." Dee passed forward her phone, selecting an entry.

"We've got you. Just relax here."

Dee jumped at an unpleasant shriek from the side of the room. "What will I do?" Betty howled.

Someone with the nametag of Sonic Might came forward, slowly, their cane tapping against the floor. "You like the cops, right? Call them." And as the cane vibrated, suddenly Betty could no longer be heard, whatever sounds she was making contained within her web.

As another hero waved from next to a table, the entire tangle of Floating Betty in her web was moved out, into the hallway, and the doors again shut.

"Dee?" a voice asked softly, next to her. "Your friend is on the way. Could you tell me, what was it you were asking about the bread?"

HOLD STEADY AGAINST THE TIDE

BY BEATRICE MORGAN

CN: Flooding during a storm; parent's ill health

The lilac cyclamen on Rosemary's windowsill unfurled from its miserable droop as she stepped into the room and softly closed the door. She greeted each of her plants individually, her voice low to avoid disturbing her mother resting in the next room. The vines trailing from her bookcase encircled her left wrist; when she stroked a finger down the centre of a leaf, the vine caressed her palm in return.

Communicating with the plants took more effort with her left arm, because the connection between her brain and her mechanical hand was slower, like talking with a mouth full of treacle. Despite this, she could feel the vine's simmering distress.

97

HOLD STEADY AGAINST THE TIDE

"There," Rosemary whispered, "it won't be so bad here. There's no need to worry, you're safe."

None of her plants enjoyed the upheaval of the cross-country move, but they had no choice in their relocation. Just like Rosemary had no choice but to close her plant nursery and fill her mother's spare bedroom with what little she could save. But if she could decide to make the most of it, they could put up with it too.

An alarming groan echoed through the open window from the direction of the seafront. Rosemary startled, banging her elbow on the corner of a bookshelf. There were sounds Rosemary expected from a coastal town, like screaming seagulls and rushing waves, but that wasn't one of them. Clutching her throbbing elbow, she padded out to where her mother curled under a thick blanket on the sofa. "Are you asleep yet?" she asked under her breath.

Her mother cracked an eye, the other pressed shut by the cushion lodged under her face. "Not if you need me."

Rosemary had moved here because her mother needed her, rather than the other way around, but breaking forty years of habit must be difficult.

"That noise, what was it?" Rosemary asked.

"Hmm?"

"The groan-crack-thing. It frightened the living daylights out of me."

It was the tidal defences, her mother explained. They were a series of barriers that pivoted on the fortnightly spring tides which surged so high that without intervention they would flood the town. The defences were supposed to be a feat of wizardly engineering controlled by sophisticated technology, but sometimes individual barriers fell out of sync.

"That's when they make all that noise. Grinding against each other all wrong, I suppose. And it's been getting worse. More things going wrong. Not two months ago, a whole stretch of them opened up a day too early, and the drainage system downtown got an unpleasant, real-time test."

Of all the things Rosemary had to worry about, the precarity of living at sea-level wasn't a welcome addition to the list.

It played on her mind as she made dinner: there was everything she knew to expect, like the stress of caring for her ailing mother, and the frustration of tying up a decade of business from a distance; but there was also everything she didn't know she needed to worry about, like dubiously successful sea defences and, apparently, an uncooperative cooker. She tapped the temperature icon again, but still nothing happened.

It took several tries before she realised it wasn't registering her prosthetic hand. An irritating oversight, since her arm and the cooker were both supposed to be cutting-edge and intuitive–she would settle for robust enough to deal with actual reality.

Finally, the soup started bubbling, but then her arm produced several hefty pulses that sent her shoulder into spasm, at the same time as the cooker viciously dialled up the temperature unprompted. Half the soup was burned to the bottom of the pan before she had the upper body control to remove it from the heat.

When her mother came to investigate the acrid smell, she made a comforting noise, as though Rosemary was four instead of forty-three. "You spent all yesterday travelling," she said, ushering Rosemary towards the front door. "And you've been cooped up today. You need to get some fresh air."

HOLD STEADY AGAINST THE TIDE

Fresh air wouldn't make dinner edible, but Rosemary accepted her jacket and a reminder that they were close to famous wetlands. That's how the coastline here was talked about: famous! Beautiful! The reason the town existed in the first place, since it grew from a fishing village nestled on the estuary. So she followed the brackish scent to the break where buildings melted into glorious saltmarsh.

Or, at least, that's what was supposed to happen. Instead, the buildings crumbled away to heartbreak. The saltmarsh was a shadow of what she'd been promised, and Rosemary was confronted by more suffering than she'd ever encountered before—and she's known many suffering plants in her time.

Sharp wind sliced tear tracks deeper into her cheeks as she followed the boardwalk towards the blue-green skyline. There were interactive information signs placed periodically, for tourists treasure-hunting factoids about what the wetlands used to be. She stepped off the path to kneel by a tuft of sea-spurrey. The treacle connection through her left hand was useful this time since it muted the painful cries. The leaves were brown-tinged instead of vibrant. It was trapped in a half-life, a purgatory of oil-poisoned water and gradual erosion. So far from thriving but not the release of a swift death either.

Rosemary tried to give the people of the town the benefit of the doubt. Perhaps, when plants were merely plants, it was difficult to tell the difference between a happily mud-bound sprawl of seaspurrey and scurvygrass and seepweed, and the neglected, decaying equivalent. She tried, but this was close to unforgivable. She once ended a relationship after cut flowers left her feeling like she'd been gifted a bundle of nearly-corpses, and that was just a handful, not an entire stretch of marshland.

Rosemary stroked fleshy leaves of the sea-spurrey and spoke lovingly; she watched it stand taller, and a sprig of green sprang from a bare patch of mud nearby. It was somehow even worse to know that all this wetland needed was care. Or, at least, the absence of wilful disregard.

It took effort to poison salt-grown lives.

Rosemary started to spend the duration of her mother's afternoon naps on walks to the saltmarsh. For an hour every day she would sit among the plants and give them tenderness. Hope. Patch by patch, they grew a little stronger, a little sturdier, although she wasn't able to bring the water back to the most inland stretch of once-saltmarsh that had long since been drained away. Her particular aptitudes only related to the plants themselves, not the surrounding waterways or properties of the soil. She could coax roots into shifting silt, which could divert a rising tide to where it was most urgently needed, but this had to be done incrementally. To attempt such an endeavour all at once would require more energy than she had to spare.

It had taken Rosemary many years to finely-hone her aptitude. Communication was the easy part—like asking after a neighbour's day. Influence was much trickier to finesse. During teenage growthspurts she had to avoid particularly verdant areas, since they would burst into overgrowth the moment her attention wandered. At times she would drain her energy into a plant until she collapsed; other times she could not even pass enough to unfurl a new leaf.

But her years working in plant nurseries, especially running her own, sharpened her control, and she reaped the benefits out on the marsh. There was nothing she did so well as coaxing new life out of soil and bolstering life that was flagging. She came home to care for her mother, but her heart had room for more besides, so she filled it.

A fortnight after her arrival, another spring tide passed, and then another. The barriers held.

In the quiet moments when her mother was resting, Rosemary learned more about the tide barriers: how they were only five years old; how they were built by people with considerable engineering aptitudes when rising seas brought the highest tides higher than most of the town; how no-one had wanted to block the waves more permanently because the town manifested from a working estuary and ships needed to move freely for three-quarters of the month. They were controlled by such advanced systems that no human oversight was needed. Though necessary, Rosemary thought them horizon-scarring.

One morning a parcel arrived, marked with purple handwriting reading *FRAGILE* and *This Way Up*. Rosemary didn't wait until the afternoon to transport its contents to the seafront. Though she'd left the plant trade, she still had contacts, and one of them was an ethical source of a rare samphire species that should be present on the saltmarsh but wasn't—she'd spent two days searching, just in case.

It took as long to satisfy the legality, since it was a protected and regulated species, but she didn't mind. Even without her particular aptitudes she would care about prioritising ethical interactions with wild specimens: it was the most important thing she learned on field trips as a student. (Except perhaps proper wound care, since it was bacteria acquired through broken skin on such a trip which destroyed the flesh of her left arm.) The trade of this samphire was so tightly regulated because its rarity emerged from a perfect storm: it was a culinary delicacy; it was difficult to propagate and only grew well in the wild; its habitats were disappearing beneath encroaching seas. Merely handling it felt like an honour.

Though she tried to tend to the whole marsh equally, this samphire was her favourite; she often lingered a little longer with her encouragement, watching as new shoots burst from the mud. The first time she saw a flower nestled among the waxy leaves she cried, and her tears were only slightly sad this time.

On one of her mother's more difficult days—when the pain was untouchable—Rosemary wouldn't leave her for an afternoon, waiting instead until she finally succumbed to fatigue as the sky purpled. Not a particularly safe decision, and Rosemary had to activate the torch built into her prosthetic arm as clouds roiled in to intercept the final dregs of sunlight, but she didn't need to see the marsh, only feel it. The barriers interrupted the inky horizon at intervals, not yet pivoted closed despite the coming spring tide and the surges of a forecast storm. Without instruction her feet carried her towards the samphire, where beams of light already danced.

The samphire screamed.

"Hey!" Rosemary yelled, breaking into a jog, "what do you think you're doing?"

Two shadowed figures scrambled to gather the bags of dug-up samphire. If they'd come under the cover of darkness, they knew as well as she did that harvesting this rare species was illegal.

"I won't report you," she begged at their retreat, because she wanted the best outcome more than she wanted to scratch out their eyes, "if you just put it back. Please, just put it back."

One of the poachers threw a two-fingered salute over their shoulder. Neither of them turned back.

HOLD STEADY AGAINST THE TIDE

Her rage was incandescent.

Rosemary had devoted weeks to growing that samphire. She switched the torch in her arm to wide-beam to survey the damage, and the light was fractured by the first drops of rain. The poachers had destroyed half the samphire's hard work in one fell swoop. There were empty craters where entire plants had been dug up; others were ruthlessly slain to stubs. She would scream if she hadn't run the air from her lungs.

Dropping to a crouch Rosemary dug her fingers into the mud around one of the remaining plants so her fingers were touching the roots, but when she tried to open a connection, she couldn't focus on healing. On growth. Her anger and betrayal bubbled like acid and the samphire hissed, crackling brown at the edges. Rosemary recoiled as though she was the one burned, not the samphire. She directed a breath in through her nose and out through her mouth, her hands hugged to her chest to stop them causing any more harm—and to point the light to the sky so she didn't have to see the scars left by the poachers and by her rage. The rain on her lips tasted sour.

The next morning Rosemary brooded as one cacophony of thunder after another rattled the back door like an unwelcome guest. Her mother knew better than to interrupt her bad mood, so Rosemary could tell it was serious when she shuffled in, the phone held aloft.

"Hannah called." This was her mother's friend, the one who lived on the banks of the estuary. "The barriers were supposed to close last night. But they didn't."

Outside, the wind whistled like a baleful piper.

"What does that mean?" Rosemary asked, but her mother just shook her head and touched a knuckle to her chin, sinking abruptly into the nearest chair. If a spring high tide in good weather could flood the town, Rosemary could conjure a hundred scenarios of the sea combining forces with the storm, and none of them were pleasant.

The weather worsened as lunchtime approached, the percussion of the rain only interrupted by evermore threatening thunder. High tide would arrive by mid-afternoon, but still she checked and double checked the tide tables in case the miraculous was possible. Then a rumble rent the air, a terrible noise caught between the crack of collapsing metal and the cry of a tree torn up by the roots.

"Was that thunder?" Rosemary demanded, even though she knew it wasn't. Her mother's phone rang. It was Hannah again.

"Someone tried to manually override the barrier controls," her mother said, the phone still pressed to her ear. "It broke. Or there was a collision—they shouldn't be able to collide," came her distressed aside, "and the port authorities aren't communicating. They say it's someone else's responsibility, but there isn't anybody else."

If they had no barriers to hold back the tide, and no one coordinating an emergency response, they were screwed. Rosemary's eye caught on her boots on the doormat, still mud-glazed from the night before. Despite the poacher's gouging, the wetlands were stronger than they'd been for years. This coastline was protected long before the port authority did or didn't build those barriers. Rosemary sprang up, snatching her coat from the rack. Over her mother's protests she said,

"Hannah's lived in that neighbourhood for a long time? She knows her neighbours?" Her mother nodded. "She needs to let everyone know what's happening, and corral anyone who doesn't have transportation of their own–does she have a car?" Another nod. "They need to get inland before there's any more water on the roads."

Part of her—most of her—wanted to stay and look after her mum. She fought that instinct, because her mother had enough sense to shelter upstairs and hunker down through the storm. She wanted her mum's survival more than anything, and this was the best way to fight for it. Rosemary was the only one with particular aptitudes that could protect all of them, not just her mother, from the oncoming carnage.

Rosemary ran and ran and didn't stop even when her burning lungs cried for gasps of rain-drenched air that choked her. The sky was grey. The downpour lashed in sheets of grey. The sea writhed grey and malicious through the saltmarsh as Rosemary pounded down the boardwalk, further inshore than she'd ever seen it. She threw herself into the swirling mud.

It sucked her in up to her calves and tried to hold her fast; she called to the surrounding roots to shift the silt strangle-hold until she could take a step, then another. Finally, she reached a patch held stable by stubborn vegetation, sunk only as far as her ankles.

And then she screamed.

The howling wind stole her voice so she fell to her knees, dug her fingers into the mud and screamed again—so the plants could feel if they could not hear. As it rippled out from her, they answered her call-to-arms, the sea-spurrey and scurvygrass and seepweed. If they could hold steady, the sea would lose its power to the plants' interference and the threat of flooding would dissipate before it could reach the town.

Another terrifying groan. The useless, useless barriers crying havoc. A wave breached the bank of silt and plants, washing freezing water over Rosemary's legs. She gasped but did not let go.

With each new wave the water level crept higher. High tide was still hours away. Her mechanical arm threatened to resist submersion.

She held on. She held on. She held on.

Drenched to the skin, Rosemary weakened. The cold water leached energy as quickly as her efforts to bolster the marsh. Her toes were numb. Her face was numb. Her knees left like they belonged to another person entirely. But she poured everything she could into raising the vegetation higher, into holding the mud firm between intractable roots. This saltmarsh was the last defence—had always been the last defence—so she held on.

The merciless sea buffeted her as it rose, and she had a sudden, sickening vision of drowning. Smothered by silt and saltwater. Sucked out with the tide as soon as it started retreating.

But as her exhausted body lurched with the tug of the waves, something grabbed her ankles, held them still. Something else formed around her torso, lifting her upright so her face wouldn't slip under a swell. The sea-spurrey, scurvygrass, seepweed, samphire, previously swaying with the waves, now unflinchingly still. The saltmarsh cradled her. She channelled every last drop of her strength into their fight.

She spared a glance over her shoulder, squinting through the rain to distinguish the churning water from the churning everything else. She told herself it was working, partly because there was no other option, but mostly because it looked like it was true.

HELL WEEK

BY EMMA HARDY

CN: Death, negative self-talk

I'm doing it again. Pushing at the "pull" door so hard the hinges snap and bend, and it's almost like a two-way swing door, except when I let go, the cracked and bent hinges lock in place and now the door's just open.

"I'm so sorry," I say to the teenage barista behind the counter. "I don't know my own strength."

"It says pull," she tells me, disgruntled, as though I haven't already noticed. As though I hadn't also heard the screech and crack of metal against metal and figured it out myself.

"Let me replace it," I say. The government has a fund for things like this.

HELL WEEK

My day is already ruined. Now I'll have to fill out one of those online forms, talk to whoever is working at Town Hall today, remind them that *yes, the funding is for any super-strength related incident, no it's not only for life-and-death situations and yes, I'm up-to-date with my G.O.O.D. G.U.Y. trainings.* It's not even nine o'clock.

"Holy shit," says the teenager behind the counter, but she's looking at me now instead of the door. "You're from TikTok. Hell Week, yeah?"

I shrug like *yes* and give her a smile, even though I'm not feeling it.

"The girls at school are *not* going to believe me," she says, and asks for a photo. I say yes and wrap my arm around her shoulder to get in close. She flinches.

"Sorry," I say, hand jumping off her.

She laughs and rubs her shoulder like the whole thing's funny, then snaps a selfie where I'm just smiling next to her instead. I look worn out in the photo, like my smile's half-asleep, but she doesn't notice. (She only checks it to make sure she looks good.)

I grab a seat by the window, pulling the chair out gently. I've had enough accidents for the day. I sense the teenager behind the counter recording me, probably sending a video to her friends, and I feel my gears all ground up the wrong way.

Here, I text Palavi. *Hurry upppppppp.*

Palavi is late as usual, but I wait for her before I order a coffee. She comes in quarter-past-nine and smooches my brow.

"What's up with the door?" she says and sits down next to me. "You better hope a school burns down. The government's going to want to see some serious rescuing for all the money you're costing them, Ter—sorry, Hell Week."

"Whatever," I tell her, as she weaves her fingers through mine. I'm in no mood to make light. "You're late."

"Okay," she says, drawing out the vowels like she's talking to a child. "You're grumpy. Have you checked *Flo*?" I untangle my fingers from hers.

"I'm allowed to be grumpy," I tell her. "It doesn't have to mean *that's* happening."

She gives me a look like she's either worried or annoyed. I'm reading too much into it.

"Humour me," she says. "Check."

"Fine," I say. I pull out my phone. The screen is cracked and the sides are all wonky from where I've squeezed it too hard. It unlocks when it sees my face and I swipe through the screens. I'm going as gentle as possible, but my whole body's buzzing. A shard of glass snaps off the bottom of the screen and cracks onto the floor.

"Careful," says Palavi.

"I *am* being careful," I snap back.

I open Flo and deflate: four days until my period. I rest my forehead against the table. I can feel my heartbeat in my ears.

"Whatever," I say into the wooden tabletop. "Doesn't mean I'm not pissed off."

She doesn't even say *I told you so*. She just tangles her hand back through mine and says, "I know. We'll take it easy the next few days."

∎ ·−∎ · ∎∎·−·∎ · · · ∎∎∎

At home, I snap a Prozac in half and take it. The back of my right knee aches. Even the cat is ignoring me. When we came in, I tried to pet her, but she gave me one sniff and bolted. I've been lying on the couch since, scrolling through my old TikToks. I hate my chipper can-do attitude. She doesn't seem like the real me: so happy, so fake. I lock my phone and throw an arm across my face. I can hear Palavi doing the dishes and I don't understand why she has to be so loud about it. I'm worked up over nothing, but that doesn't mean I'm not worked up.

"Hey," Palavi calls across the room, "Roma asked if I wanna go to White Night with them tonight. You mind?"

"I don't want to go out," I say from the couch, and make a disparaging gesture towards my womb. "Remember?" Palavi's half-looking at her phone, half-looking at me.

"You don't have to come," she says.

"Whatever," I say. Sometimes I feel like I'm playing it up—how stroppy I feel—but I do it anyway.

Palavi bites her lip like she's gonna say something, but just shakes her head instead. Then: "I know you don't want to hear it, but it'll pass."

"Just because I'm PMDDing doesn't mean my feelings aren't real," I say.

Palavi nods, tells me that she knows, and says that she's going to go anyway. I think she must hate me.

"This doesn't mean I hate you," Palavi says. "It means I want a night with my friend. I'll come back here after. We'll cuddle."

She says that she loves me. She says it will be nice for me to have a night to myself. And because I know she's going anyway, I say okay.

When she leaves, I squeeze my pillow so hard that the memory foam doesn't bounce back.

■ ▪ ■ ■ ▪ ■ ■ ▪ ▪ ▪ ■ ■ ▪ ▪ ▪ ■ ■ ■ ■

I watch re-runs of *MythBusters* just to feel less lonely. I like the bald guy: I like his little beret, his slow, calm way of speaking. My body lulls into a slow, numb kind of calm, so I google *how long does PMDD last* just to make myself miserable. An article about Premenstrual Dysphoric Disorder pops up. The word *dysphoric*, it says, stems from the Greek δυσ, meaning evil, and φέρω, to carry. An evil to carry. The Greeks were so dramatic.

A pop-up asks—*Was this information useful?*—and I click no just because.

The cat still won't come near me, so I lie in bed, skipping through Snaps of everyone at White Night. They've lit up Fed Square like a Gotye video on acid. Roma's posted a video of Palavi in front of a huge light-show serpent weaving its way through gum trees. The lights make it look like she's in another universe. I press my finger against the screen to hold the moment a little longer, and the screen cracks and glitches beneath me.

My phone vibrates and a banner pops down. It's Palavi: *Is that you??? WTF????*

I sit up in bed, tap the message—not even to respond—just to see if I read it right. I hear the beginnings of movement from the doorway. At first, I think it's the cat, come to make amends, but then the room glows bright white, and a shadow fills the doorframe.

I jump to my feet. My arms snap up to shield my eyes, it takes a moment for the glow to fade and my eyes to adjust. When I lower my arms, I see myself in the door frame—only I'm not myself, I'm broad and muscular with bright red hair down to my ass. My skin is glowing, clear. My ass is huge, practically bursting out of the red short-shorts I'm wearing. It's a boulder of muscle. My ass isn't that big.

"Who are you?" I ask the bulging figure in the doorframe.

"I'm you, obviously," she says, and her voice sounds like my voice, only chipper, fake. "Come on, we need to move."

"You're not me," I say. Her skin is too firm. Her waist too thick. She's too strong to be me.

She pulls up her short-shorts and shows me a small purple birthmark on her left butt cheek. It looks like an over-ripe kalamata olive. I have the exact same one, only hers shimmies and dances as the muscles in her legs twitch and flex. I feel my throat rise with something rancid.

"I'm you if you went to med school," she says. "Which we did—at least, in my universe. They call me Rock."

"As in *The* Rock?" I ask. Her expression stays blank.

"Well, yeah," she chirps. "I guess you could say I'm the Rock."

"You can't be here," I say. Inter-universe travel is illegal. It had been too much bureaucracy: heroes on their stag nights smashing up neighbouring universes and blaming their alter-egos. Too hard to keep track.

"I know," she says. For a moment, her smile dims. "Unfortunately, we didn't listen."

She grabs my phone, pulls up a livestream, and turns it to face me. Through the cracks and glitches, I see another version of myself, glowing red, fists clenched, smashing the concrete beneath me with my feet. The footage shakes and stumbles. Tinny screams echo through the phone's speakers.

"Shit," I say.

"I know," the same voice echoes back.

■ ▪■ ▪ ■■▪·▪■ ▪▪▪ ▪■ ■■

The Rock and I are running down Swanston Street. My phone's dinging and buzzing in my waistband. Everyone's running the other way, away from the river. One man sees us, squeals, and stumbles in panic, then launches himself into a Boba Tea shop.

"I can't be out," I tell Rock, panting. I'm not built for cardio. "It's *that time*, if you get me."

She looks at me, smiling and serene. Her muscles bulge as she moves. Her breath is steady. A real hero.

"The world doesn't have to stop because you're about to get your period," she says. I hate how kind she sounds. How not-me she sounds. "That's internalised patriarchy speaking."

"Right," I say through my teeth. "It's all in my head."

"I don't mean it that way," she says. "We all have our own stuff to work through."

I want to tell her that I'm too strong to risk it, too scared of what I'm capable of, but it's an absurd thing to say to myself, let alone a self as strong as her.

"Besides," she says, all chipper again. "We need you."

I run faster. The pavement cracks like early morning sand beneath my feet.

"I'm sure *you* can handle it," I say.

Rock furrows her brow, matches my pace.

"Tried that in the last universe she went to," she says. "I didn't belong there, either. It didn't count. I could hold her for a little while, but since neither of us had any roots in that universe, nothing I did to her really counted. When I killed her, she just zapped back to her old universe."

She looks at me, puffed and struggling next to her, and can tell I'm not following.

"When an action can't be grounded in the time and place of that world, it messes with the temporal reality of those events. It's like dying in a dream. If killing her is gonna stick, you need to be the one to do it. It has to be real *here—in this universe—to stop her.*"

Rock grows tired of my pace. She scoops me up, cradles me like a baby, and runs faster. I'm limp and light in her arms.

"And anyway," Rock says. I can feel her voice buzz in her chest. "She's looking for you."

■·■■ ·■■·-■■·--■■■■

When we get to Fed Square, Rock lowers me to the pavement. It's quiet. My limbs are soggy noodles. Legs ache and not even from running.

"She's here," she says.

I look but can't see anyone. Only the lights, brighter in person, shimmering and dancing across Fed Square's broad geometric shapes. I don't notice the people at first: crouched shadows behind the tram shelter, the silhouettes of feet beneath the fast food counters across the road.

Then, a smash: "Fuck you, Hell Week."

I turn towards the voice. She's walking straight through the plaza, up from Birrarung Marr. The gum trees behind her dance with red light. She's glowing red too: her hair, her skin. She looks soft, at first, until I notice the sharp splinters of her eyes.

"Terror," Rock warns. "Go home before it's too late."

But Terror doesn't listen. She keeps walking towards us. I feel dazed. I want to run, want to hide. Worst of all, I want to fight. I imagine digging my fingers into her sharp little eyes, popping them like blisters. I feel my nails crack and break against the skin of my palms. I take a breath, unclench my fists.

"Okay," Rock says. "You've got this."

Terror lunges forward and kicks through a concrete bench.

Cement shatters and lights the air with dust.

"Fuck you," is all she says.

She swoops toward me, fists raised.

I duck and cower.

Rock rushes forward, bounds over my crouched body, elbows Terror in the neck.

I stay hunched low, watch my two selves fight and don't want anyone to win. Rock slams Terror to the ground, shatters the pavement. Terror just glows redder. Red with rage and blood.

"Fuck you," my voices echo through the square. Can't tell that it's not me speaking.

Terror drags herself up and lobs a flaccid punch at Rock. It's useless. Rock catches the punch, pulls Terror's arm behind her back, and I watch myself in another self's grip.

"Come on," Rock yells. Her voice is hard now. Cold. No longer fake-chipper. "We need you."

I scramble toward my entwined bodies. When I get close, Terror squirms back, hurls a mouthful of spit at my face.

"Fuck you," she says again.

I don't think. I slap her face sideways. She spits blood all over those tiny red short-shorts.

"Bitch," Terror says, sniffling the gore from her nose. "You know I'm doing the right thing. Wiping you out of this universe. Of *every* universe."

I slap her again. Harder. I think about all the government forms I'm going to have to fill out because of her. I don't want to say she's right.

Rock's struggling to hold her still.

"Kill her," she says, pinching Terror's arms tighter behind my— no, *her*—back. Terror's face twists ugly with pain. I watch the way her lungs pulse her chest. She's breathing as fast as a heartbeat, frantic, delirious. I see her breath and feel my own match pace. It takes me a moment to catch it, to slow down, shut my eyes and fill my lungs slowly, slowly.

When I open my eyes, they're both on the ground. Writhing. Slithering.

I look down and see my face dripping blood: red like my hair, my eyes.

I lift my foot. I slam it down.

I knock the Rock unconscious.

■ ·■■ · ■■·· ■ · ·· ■■■■

My phone's buzzing and all lit up. Palavi's picture is on the screen. I press the green button and the screen splits in two.

"Terra," Palavi says. My real name. "Oh god, I thought it was really you."

The video's still loading into focus. Her face is just a mush of pixels.

"Come help," I say. "I can't carry her alone."

■ ·■■ · ■■·· ■ · ·· ■■■■

By the time Palavi finds us, I'm half-way home and Rock's almost come to. Terror is limp, quiet, barely moving. I've barely even touched her. She's a zombie beside me, half-dissociated.

Palavi pulls up and pushes open the passenger-side door. I slump Rock in the front, head against the dashboard, then lead Terror to the back. She gets in, sits, stares straight ahead.

"Hey," I say. She keeps her eyes straight.

I take her hand. It's small, like mine, the nails bitten and jagged at the ends. She doesn't flinch when I squeeze it tight.

■ ·■■ · ■■·· ■ ··· ■■■■

"She's not you," Palavi tells me when we get home. Rock is on the couch, hunched forward, nursing her head. Terror's in the other room, curled up in my bed, head on my misshapen pillow.

"I know," I say.

"I can't tell what you're thinking," Palavi says. I want to tell her it's because I'm not thinking, not really, not in any real way, but she already knows that.

"I need to sit with her," I say.

Palavi starts the kettle, and I move down the hall, towards the square of light from my bedroom door.

"Sorry I smashed up your universe," Terror says when I sit down at the end of the bed. Her voice is cracked and muffled by a pillow.

"You're kind of a bitch for that," I say.

"I'm not me," she says. "I don't think I'm me."

She rolls onto her back. Her face is puffy and scabbed. Her eyes are still red, only now they're slick with tears. I hate looking at her, hate the parts that look like me.

"You don't have to be happy," I tell her. "But you do have to be less shit."

We sit like that—her silently staring at the ceiling, me just staring at her, getting used to it—until Palavi comes in and puts two cups of tea on the bedside table.

"No one died," says Palavi. I wonder how she knows. She holds up her phone, no scratches, no dents: "Live updates."

Terror makes a breath that means something—I don't know what—and Palavi sits down on the mattress next to me. She squeezes Terror's foot through the blanket.

"You know," she says. "Eliminating yourself from every single universe isn't even the wildest thought you've had."

Terror sits up a little, looks at her, and I can see the realisation click. It's like that with Palavi. I've never seen anyone get angry when they realise, she can read their mind. It's comforting, if anything, knowing she's in there too. Sometimes I think that's her real superpower.

"I know you don't want to hear this," says Palavi. "But it always passes. You just need to find a way to sit with the discomfort until it does."

Terror doesn't say anything, just looks at Palavi for a while, and Palavi nods, and says I know, I know, and slowly, slowly, Terror's body relaxes back into the pillows.

"You're no different in this universe." It's Rock. She's leaning against the doorframe, looking at Palavi. The cat's come out of hiding. She's rubbing her slick little black body against Rock's legs, tail high in the air. "You can't make excuses for someone who's fucked up."

Palavi cuts her a look. My least favourite look. It's the look she gave me the first time I ever lied to her; the last time I ever lied to her. "You should focus on the excuses you make for yourself," she says.

"I don't need excuses," says Rock. There's bitterness to her tone. I wonder if I've knocked the chipper out of her.

"Don't try with me," says Palavi. "You're making up for your mistakes, too. You can hide it in your universe, but not from me."

Rock puts a hand to her head, doesn't say anything. She stares at Palavi for a while. The cat's still running circles through her legs, acting desperate. Rock lifts her chin, says, "This universe is getting thin. I'm going back."

She pulls a small device, no bigger than a USB, from the waistband of her short-shorts and turns her back to us. The hallway glows white, and then she's gone. The cat lets out one long, betrayed yowl. She looks at the empty hallway, then at us, and stalks away, disinterested.

It's only us and Palavi now. I slip into bed next to them and, like Palavi promised, we stay that way until morning.

CAPTAIN MAVEN AND THE ICE QUEEN

BY JAMIESON WOLF

Captain Maven stood looking down at the city.

Standing on the roof of headquarters was where he did his best thinking. The lights of the city made Ottawa look as if it were covered in a blanket of stars, and there was something about the sound of the wind and traffic down below that quieted him. It was at these moments that he was the most centered.

He heard the click and slam of the roof access door and then a voice rang out through the air: "You look moody as fuck."

Maven's partner Gregory came to stand beside him, looking beautiful in the evening light. His dark hair was blown by the wind and the moonlight shone in his blue eyes, making them look like glass. Maven traced Gregory's jaw, forever covered in stubble and his mouth was curved in a sardonic grin.

"Thanks, babe. You didn't have to come all the way up here."

"I know, but then I would have missed out on the sight of you look all sexy and tortured." Gregory said. "I like the new cape by the way. The extra sparkles are sure to help you blend into the darkness." He leaned in and kissed Maven. "How are you doing?" Gregory had been asking that a lot lately.

He had every right to be concerned, but Maven wished people would ask him something different. Didn't they have anything better to ask him? Maven rubbed his chest self-consciously. Even now, he could feel the shadow man awake within him and did everything he could to ignore his presence.

He'd read stories of mediums that were possessed by ghosts and spirits where the spirit was able to take over their bodies; of course, a lot of those reports were debunked as myths. With Maven, this was the truth. He *did* have another being inside of him, a being known as Max Shadow. He just wasn't sure which one of them had control of his body nowadays.

Maven looked out at the city of Ottawa below him and thought of what his life had been like before MS and it had seemed so simple, really. Being able to get up every day and save the city without a care about his body. Now, he had to force his body to do everything; Max Shadow was able to take over totally some days.

Gregory was looking at him, still waiting for a response. Maven sighed inwardly. "I'm fine," he said.

For a second, Gregory looked like he wanted to smack Maven.

"For fuck sakes Arnold, you could at least be honest with me." The fact that Gregory refused to call him Captain Maven had bothered him at first, but now it was a reminder that Gregory was an anchor in a world filled with bullshit.

"The fact that it took you that long to answer me tells me that you're inside yourself again. You spend entirely too much time there. You could let me draw you out a bit, okay?"

Maven leaned closer and kissed him. "Okay," he said. "Thank you."

The communicator on Maven's wrist started to beep and flash. Looking at it, Maven saw two words: *Control Room*.

"Looks like something else has arrived to get you out of your own head," Gregory said.

■ ·■■ · ■ ■·· ·■ ■ ··· ■ ■ ■■

They arrived in the control room to find almost everyone there already.

Finley Braveheart stood in front of the computer console with Tara Dawn, and they were both watching something on the screen with their mouths hanging open. Sandoz and Carley looked as if they would both be ill and Tiando held Dez in a hug, their bodies turned away from the screen.

Maven opened his mouth to ask what the problem was, but then he looked up at the viewscreen and felt the ground underneath him shift. Inside, Max Shadow screamed in triumph. Maven could feel Max Shadow smiling and anything that made that asshole happy was bad.

On the screen in front of him, Maven watched a face he had never wanted to see again smile broadly and for a moment, Maven thought she could see him through the screen but then he remembered that she always wore that look when she was creating mayhem. Countless people ran away from her, and they watched as sheets of ice began to form on the ground, making escape impossible. Shards of ice fell from the sky and the mortals in danger did everything they could to protect themselves.

"I never thought I'd see her again," Dez said, a note of panic in his voice. They all knew what had happened. The last time they had fought the Ice Queen, she had used Dez's own water powers against him and frozen the water inside of him. He'd almost died.

"Why's that?" Gregory said. He was the odd man out; not being a superhero, he'd never fought her.

"Because she's supposed to be dead." Maven said.

He stared at the screen and the memory of when they had fought her last flashed into his mind. Maven could see the killing blow, watched as Finley slammed into her and then Maven used the light from his sceptre to melt her like the wicked witch that she was. He remembered the puddle, the only thing that remained of her, and how it reflected the light on its surface.

"Well, I hate to tell you," Gregory said. "She seems pretty alive on the screen. Only the good die young right? Besides, don't the evil villains always come back? Who's that she's with anyways?"

They looked at the screen again and saw that the Ice Queen was indeed with someone who burned as bright as the sun.

"Solar Flare!" Carley said. Her voice sounded grim compared to its usual relaxed tones. Carley Bravo could help calm the mood of anyone around her, and it looked like she could use some of her own powers right now.

"You look a little tense, Carley," Tianado said, giving her a grin.

He wore all black and his black eyes could strike fear in people when his gaze was locked on theirs. It didn't help that he could bring eternal darkness to a room, no matter how well lit it was. He also had a very sarcastic sense of humour. "Care for a tea? It's herbal."

"Fuck you very much." She stuck her tongue out at him. "He's supposed to be dead, *too!*"

"Well, then I'd say you all have a mission," Gregory said. "What's that, mister knows it all?" Tianado asked.

"We have to find them before they find us," Maven said.

■ ·■ ■ · ■ ■·· ■ ■ ·· · ■ ■ ■

Tara got to work right away, clicking around on the computer trying to see what she could find. Sandoz and Dez flipped through the news channels and Carley listened to the police scanner.

"They're at York and Clarence in the Byward Market." Carley said. She looked up at the screen. "See? They are making progress. In the video we saw before, they are on Bank Street. They're on the move, but for what?"

As Sandoz and Dez continued clicking through channels, Maven thought it was like watching a flipbook: They were on Bank Street, they were in Confederation Park, they were terrorizing people at the Chateau Laurier; but they weren't *doing* anything, not really. They were on the move, and they were causing a lot of havoc, but their actions didn't have any real intent. Maven watched them and wondered why they were focusing everything in the downtown core.

His cup of power shook at his side. It had been doing this a lot lately to get his attention. Maven looked down at it and detached it from his belt. The cup could let him see into different parts of Ottawa and could even act as a portal to the location of the person that he could see through the cup. Tara often referred to it as his Romper Room mirror; Maven didn't appreciate the humour.

Taking the cup from his belt, he looked into it. He saw the Ice Queen and Solar Flare looking at a map. Solar Flare was unfurling it on a table and the Ice Queen was randomly choosing spots on the map with little icicles, jammed into the map like pushpins. Maven knew that he was seeing something that had already happened, that the spots they were going to terrorize had already been chosen. He could see icicles on the map and they formed a line.

Maven looked up from the cup of power. "They are trying to draw us out," he said quietly.

Dez flipped to another channel and Solar Flare turned to smile at the camera, his eyes filled with a light that was almost brighter than the sun from which he took his name. The Ice Queen seemed to be dancing across in front of the hotel, shooting out ice with increasing regularity. The havoc it caused lacked her usual style and finesse.

Even now, Solar Flare and the Ice Queen terrorized tourists in front of Rideau Centre, the Ice Queen turning the streets into ice and Solar Flare making the water catch flame, causing people to run away screaming. It seemed too theatrical and so unplanned,

"Maven? You need to come and see this."

Hearing the tone in Tara's voice, Maven hurried over. As someone who was able to put people to an enchanted sleep, Tara was normally calming and very soothing. Now she sounded urgent and worried.

When Maven saw what she was looking at, he felt the world fall around him. Max Shadow let out a triumphant yell within him and

Maven felt the control that he had over his body slip away, just a little. For a moment, Max Shadow had taken over. Rallying, Maven shoved Max Shadow back into the compartment within his mind that he normally kept him in and took a deep breath.

Gregory gave him a concerned look, but Maven waved him off. "Turn up the volume, Tara," he said.

She nodded and did so and they all gathered around the computer screen. "Where did you find this?" Maven asked.

Shaking her head, Tara shivered and said, "You don't want to know. There are some dark parts of the world, online and off." On the screen, the Ice Queen and a man shared a drink together. They clinked glasses of wine, and the Ice Queen gave the man a simpering smile. He was partially obscured by darkness, but Maven would recognize him anywhere, not just because of the roar of joy that he heard within himself. The man talking to the Ice Queen was none other than Max Shadow, but with more shape than he'd had when Maven had seen him last. In the video, Max Shadow looked almost human rather than the monster that he had become.

When the video clip went dark, Maven stared at the others, and Gregory saw something in Maven's eyes. "What are you thinking?" Maven sighed. Gregory knew him too well. "I can see the gears running in your head."

Inside of Maven, Max was still roaring with joy but that joy was filled with sadness now that they were no longer looking at the Ice Queen. The sound filled up Maven's mind so that it took him a while to find his words. He pushed Max Shadow back down within himself and when Maven spoke, his words were slow and thoughtful. "I thought that the Ice Queen was trying to call us out and I think that's part of it…"

"But not all of it?" Finley said.

"No…" Maven began to pace, his sceptre of light flashing brightly with each step, almost like it was some sort of pulse. "Not all. After seeing the video that you found, Tara, and the reaction that Max Shadow has had at seeing her, I think I know what she's doing."

"That's okay," Tianado said. "Don't tell us, just string us along like you always do. It's what we're used to from you."

Finley hit Tianado in the shoulder hard and he swore. "You may continue, Maven," Finley said.

"Well, why is the Ice Queen causing all this fuss? It's not the organized mayhem that she normally does to get *our* attention. No, it was to get *Max's* attention."

"She doesn't know that Max is now inside of you?" Carley asked. "The Ice Queen has no idea that the Max she knew is gone?"

"Apparently not, and that will be our secret weapon. She's expecting him to show up, so we're going to give her what she wants."

"Um, Maven?" Sandoz said. "There's the little problem of Max Shadow being inside of you. Don't you think that might be a problem?"

Again, Gregory could see the wheels moving inside of Maven's head and was not happy about it. "*No*, Maven. You can't."

"I have to," Maven said. "It's the only way that we can get close enough."

"Again, when you feel like cluing us in, please do," Tianado said. Finley gave his other arm a hard slap.

"He wants to *become* Max Shadow," Gregory said. "I think it's a ridiculous idea, not to mention dangerous."

"It's the only way. I mean, he's inside of me, right? I just have to let him out for a bit so that the Ice Queen is fooled, lets me get close enough."

"How will we know where they are?" Tara said. "Do we have any idea where they are going to end up?"

"That's not hard, just look at the trail they're leaving." Tara pointed to the computer and the line of places the Ice Queen and Solar Flare had already done. "If they keep going on the same route, they're going to end up at Major's Hill Park."

"Then that's where we have to go." Maven said.

■ ·■■ ·■■·· ■■ · ·· ■■■■

There was a glint in Maven's eyes that told Gregory it was pointless to try and change Maven's mind. "What happens if you get stuck as Max?" Gregory said, knowing that it was easier to just go with Maven's plans than fight against them. "What happens if you don't get your body back?"

"Then that's the price I will have to pay to keep the city safe." Maven said. He was stretching his cup of power, making its opening big enough to step into. "I know that Max likes the shadows, so he'll come out when it's dark. It's the only way."

Gregory sighed. "Do what you must, Arnold."

Maven nodded and gave Gregory a quick kiss. He stepped into the portal that waited at the bottom of his cup of power. There was a flash of bright purple light and the world around them crackled with purple electricity, glowing bright for a moment. Gregory waited, hoping that it wouldn't work, that Arnold would walk out of the portal unsuccessful. When the light faded, Max Shadow stepped out of the cup and gave everyone a big smile.

Gregory knew that it was Arnold, but he didn't look anything like the Arnold that Gregory knew. Gone were the bald head, strong chin and nice cheekbones. He looked like a different person, all shadows, blurred lines and darkness.

"That's fucking creepy," Tianado said.

"Tell me about it," Maven said.

"How does it feel?" Gregory said, unnerved by seeing Max Shadow shape Arnold's words.

"I feel disgusting, but we have to keep the people of Ottawa safe." Maven said. What he didn't say was that he had to force his body to move as if he were walking through quicksand. Having Max Shadow on the surface like this seemed to make the shadow man stronger. Maven could feel him testing the boundaries of his strength and knew that he would have to fight Max every step of the way. It was worth it as long as he saved Ottawa. "Let's go break some ice," Maven said.

■ ▪ ▪ ■ ▪ ■ ■ ▪ ▪ ■ ■ ▪ ▪ ▪ ■ ▪ ■ ■

Maven passed the entrance to Major's Hill Park.

There was no one around, but that didn't mean he wasn't being watched. He knew that Finley and Tara and everyone else was watching from inside a van nearby. He could hear them in his left ear and knew that they were watching his movements on a video screen, which was comforting, even if Maven did feel a little like a lamb heading to slaughter. Just because he was a superhero didn't mean that he was all powerful "You okay, Maven?" Tara asked.

"I'm okay," he said. "Any sign of them yet?"

"No," Dez said. "But they'll show themselves. They always did like to make an entrance. The Ice Queen was always about the razzmatazz."

Maven walked onward, toward what looked like a fountain made of glass, except it was ice. Max Shadow's excitement was palpable, and Maven could feel the thrill running through his body. "Ice Queen!" Maven called out in Max's voice. "Show yourself!"

There was a whisper of cloth and the world around Maven became colder and brighter all at once. The Ice Queen and Solar Flare were in front of Maven, giving him a menacing look. The Ice Queen's clear blue eyes flashed merrily. "Why it's my Shadow!" she purred. Sauntering over to him, the Ice Queen eyed Maven like he was a piece of candy.

"With you gone, she hooked up with *me* instead," Solar Flare said, not without some jealousy.

"The idea being that the brighter the light, the more shadows I would see." She placed a hand on Maven's arm, and he forced himself not to recoil at her freezing touch. "Didn't I tell you that I would always find you?" the Ice Queen purred.

"And find me you have," Maven said, placing his hand on her arm and holding it there. Maven knew that everyone could hear him, that they were waiting for the signal...except that it never came because Max Shadow chose that moment to take over.

"I've waited so long to see you again," Max Shadow said. "I've long waited for Ice and Shadows to dance once more."

Maven tried to take a breath for himself, to shout a warning, but he found that he couldn't make a sound. He was a prisoner in his own body.

CAPTAIN MAVEN AND THE ICE QUEEN

"I'm so glad!" the Ice Queen said, rubbing Maven's arm. She leaned in and whispered closer to his ear. "I've missed you so," "And I've missed you, my frozen delight."

Maven wretched internally. He tried again to take over his body, but Max Shadow had taken over completely. His body was no longer his own. He could feel Max Shadow vibrating with pleasure and it revolted Maven, but there was nothing he could do. When a voice spoke out behind him, Maven would have jumped if he could have moved.

"Now that's just *revolting*, you could at least get a room you know."

When Max turned, Maven saw Finley Braveheart standing there, looking like a flame in the night. Behind her was Gregory and his entire crew and it was a joy to see all of them. He had never been so frightened as he was right now and seeing all of them brought him comfort.

"What is it you all think you're going to do against us?" the Ice Queen asked with a smile. "You can't fight against the powers of ice, light and shadow combined!" She let out a tinkling laugh that sounded like ice hitting the pavement.

"See that's where you're wrong," Gregory said. "There's a lot we can do. Finley, do you want to do the honours?"

"I was hoping you would ask." Finley said, giving him a grin.

She held out her hands and jets of fire shot out of her palms. Though Maven tried to move, Max Shadow was quicker; he tried to surround the Ice Queen and form a barrier against the fire, but fire could always move through shadows like the wind and there was nothing that the Ice Queen could do against the warmth of the fire. She melted into a puddle on the pavement and Dez stepped in to use his powers over water to gather her up into the air and place her in a vial made of lead. Maven could hear the Ice Queen screaming as he placed a topper in the vial.

Solar Flare let out a yell and the air was filled with the crackle of electricity as the skies around them shone with the brightness of the sun. Maven knew this was his chance, that he had to act, but he couldn't move against Max Shadow. He screamed inside his head and felt Max Shadow retreat a little, but not enough.

Tianado stepped forward and wrapped the shadows like a lover around Solar Flare, who screamed in torment as the bright sunlight that he created was snuffed out. Sandoz stepped forward and they all watched the pavement around them beginning to crack and come free. Solar Flare screamed as the cement surrounded him, his light having no effect on it. "Fuck you!" Solar Flare said.

"No thanks," Gregory said, coming forward. "I'm spoken for."

Solar Flare gave him the finger as the concrete closed around him, and Tianado put shadows around the temporary prison thick enough that no light would ever shine through. Gregory ran to Maven and pulled the cup of power out of his back pocket.

"Do you even know how to work that?" Carley said.

"Shut up and help me stretch it out," Gregory said.

All of them came forward to help Gregory stretch out the cup and soon, a purple light pulsed from it. When it was wide enough, Gregory passed it over Maven, watching Max Shadow disappear for a moment before he brought the cup back up. When he did, Max Shadow was once again inside Maven and not on the surface.

Captain Maven slumped into his lover's arms. "I couldn't move," he said. "I had no control over my body. What am I going to do if Max Shadow takes over again?" They all knew that this was a possibility.

CAPTAIN MAVEN AND THE ICE QUEEN

Gregory looked into Captain Maven's eyes and tried to communicate everything he wanted to say. He was sometimes frustrated with the English language. It didn't have enough words to describe the worry that he lived with. "Whatever happens, we'll get through this together, Arnold."

Maven smiled at the use of his name. "You can be such a bastard, you know."

"I know. I love you." Gregory said.

"I love you, too." Maven didn't know what the future would bring, but he knew that Gregory would be by his side.

He took comfort from that even as, inside of him, Max Shadow raged.

INSTITUTING A CYCLE OF VIOLENCE

BY MATTHEW DEL PAPA

*CN: ableism, death, violence, institutional
violence, medical, military*

Goldie wasn't talking. The fourteen-year-old could be moody like that, Mitchell knew, Which just made teasing the girl all the more fun. "What's the matter?" he asked, "Cat got your tongue?"

Eyes flashing with anger Goldie slammed one twitching hand onto the tray fastened to her wheelchair and, with great effort, pointed at the symbol for 'FUCK YOU OR OFF'.

Mitchell chuckled, "Good morning to you too, sunshine."

As one of the Institution's few 'verbal' residents, it often fell on him to carry the conversation. Luckily, Mitchell excelled at talking. He couldn't help himself and he didn't much want to. Inane chatter kept people entertained and, in a place like The Louis Saint Laurent Institute for Crippled Children, entertainment was hard to find.

The staff, or at least the few who still listened after hearing him natter non-stop for almost ten years, often asked, "Do you ever stop talking or is that like your superpower?"

Goldie pointed and, hand twitching in emphasis, waited for Mitchell to read her meaning aloud: "YOU. NOT. FUNNY." That last word was spelled out slowly on the alphabetical part of her tray.

"I'm sorry," he said, having read her board upside-down with long-practised ease from his own wheelchair. "You looked so sour I couldn't help myself. Let me guess, Kate got you up this morning?" A furious nod set the teen's long golden hair flying into her face.

Kate was one of six female workers at the Saint Laurent Institute and a compulsive smoker. None of the residents enjoyed her half-assed efforts as the woman rushed through work in order to slip off and sneak a 'quick puff'. But Goldie HATED her.

This morning Kate hadn't even tied Goldie's hair back…a task that took barely a moment.

Mitchell grabbed the wooden stick he kept tucked into a purely decorative shoe and being very careful, pushed the wayward locks behind his best friend's ears. "There," he said once every strand was in place. "Beautiful, as always."

That earned him a smile. And it truly was beautiful.

■ ﹒■ ■ ﹒■ ■﹒﹒■ ■ ﹒﹒﹒ ■ ■■

General Bradley stared around the lab like he owned it—which, given the billions in Pentagon funding clandestinely funneled into the research, wasn't far from the truth.

It is a devil's bargain I have signed, Dr. Claudio Mique-Alejandro Lourdes thought, and not for the first time. He maintained a neutral expression. Careful to hide his growing disdain for the general and the bloated military-industrial complex he so perfectly embodied.

Three members of Dr. Lourdes' carefully vetted team had 'disappeared' and no one knew why. He, however, had his suspicions, and Dr. Lourdes didn't want to provide the U.S. government any reason to disappear a fourth.

Instead, he plastered on a clinical smile and offered a perfectly polite, "Welcome, General Bradley. How may we assist you today?"

The general's jowly scowl deepened at the soft-spoken courtesy.

Claudio Mique-Alejandro Lourdes and Thomas Bradley couldn't be more different. Born a penniless orphan, Dr. Lourdes had clawed his way from Venezuela's most-crowded barrio through sheer brilliance. Holding degrees in chemical engineering, genetics, and evolutionary biology, he spoke with confidence and looked every part the man of science—tall, spare, and often lost in important thought. The shorter and heavier general, in contrast, stood with a bored slouch even when at attention. Boasting a fourth-generation military pedigree and being of proud WASP stock, not to mention 'substantial means', he'd exploited every familial connection to advance his career far past his competence.

Both men, however, shared a common goal: to bring their 'Project' to fruition.

"So, Lourdes. Are we ready for human trials?"

Ignoring the missing 'doctor' and the lack of respect it represented, Claudio Mique-Alejandro Lourdes took a moment before answering, "Yes, General. I believe that is the next logical step. Unfortunately, I doubt we will find many volunteers. Not with a ninety-eight percent failure rate."

General Bradley smiled at that and said, "You leave the volunteers to me. Just prepare the Juice. I want a hundred doses readied ASAP."

■ ·■ ■ ·■ ■·· ■ ■ ··· ■ ■ ■ ■

At eighteen, Mitchell Connors was soon to leave the Institute. He wasn't happy about it, but Goldie, his closest friend, was downright distraught.

The two had formed a connection upon meeting, eight years back. Mitchell had held her hand while the then six-year-old cried herself to sleep that first night. It had been Mitchell who drew her first board and, together, they'd refined and expanded the communication device until they seemed to converse in their own secret language.

An inseparable—not to mention formidable—pair, Goldie and Mitchell were often held up as examples to newcomers. They 'behaved' and 'knew their places'…at least as far as the Administrator was concerned. Which was exactly what the teens were going for.

The Louis Saint Laurent Institute for Crippled Children cared for disabled children, the majority of whom required dedicated one on one medical assistance. The group home had eight attendants per nine-hour shift serving ninety-two residents…each with uniquely specific healthcare needs.

A worse arrangement would be hard to find.

Diagnosed with a form of muscular dystrophy before his first birthday, Mitchell ranked among the Institute's 'healthiest' children on arrival at age ten. Having used a wheelchair less than a year at that point, he'd outlived dozens of friends over the intervening decade, and watched as their beds were given to new arrivals.

Sentimentality didn't exist in institutions like Saint Laurent.

Mitchell, though bright for his age, needed to have that explained to him. Luckily, an older and more worldly-wise resident, Ritchie, recognized something in the then-newcomer and explained, "We work the Institute, so it doesn't work us." That whispered bit of advice changed how Mitchell viewed his surroundings—especially when, not long after sharing those words, eighteen-year-old Ritchie was wheeled out of Saint Laurent to parts unknown.

That incident scarred Mitchell, but he'd taken Ritchie's brief tutelage and rolled with it.

He'd brought Goldie onboard soon after she arrived and, together, the two of them endeared themselves to those in authority.

It took years of thankless effort. Goldie volunteered in the kitchens where she mixed up three big batches of orange juice, from concentrate, prior to every meal. Mitchell helped with the office, answering the phone, typing up reports, and keeping the files in order. These tasks went unpaid but not unrewarded.

For their efforts the two were given the run of the place.

So, they knew—before even the Administrator—when trouble came knocking on the Institute's front door.

■ ·■■ · ■■·· ■■ ··· ■■■■

"Children?!" Dr. Lourdes sounded horrified. "You cannot be serious?" he muttered as the vehicle passed the sign reading *The Louis Saint Laurent Institute for Crippled Children*. "It is immoral and unethical to test on children!"

INSTITUTING A CYCLE OF VIOLENCE

"Not these. They're defective," the slouching general announced as if the insulting descriptor settled things.

"But...children. Do they not have families? Rights?"

"No one cares what happens here. Not even their own parents. These kids were signed over to the government and," General Bradley gestured to his straining uniform before finishing, "I'm the government."

Claudio Mique-Alejandro Lourdes didn't like hearing that sort of dismissiveness. Trying to offer a convincing argument he said, "Are you suggesting we test a multi-billion-dollar experimental drug on cripples?"

"Who better? Being wards of the state means anything we do is nice and legal, at least according to Uncle Sam. Besides, children are easy to control and easier to motivate. And these? They're institutionalized, they live in isolation, and best of all, they're used to unpleasant medical treatments."

"These are not the healthiest subjects. What with their underlying conditions. I can only imagine the complications," Dr. Lourdes hedged. "Our carefully planned methodology...the results are certain to be skewed. The whole project, years of work, could be rendered useless."

The general smirked but just said, "None of that science mumbo jumbo will matter if the Juice does what it's supposed to. These cripples will either prove us right or die, heroically, while trying." Looking off into the distance he finished, "That's a good way to go in my books, dying for your country. American soldiers volunteer to do it every day."

These kids didn't volunteer, came the thought…but the doctor knew better than to voice his disdain too vocally. Biting back the objection, he admitted, *No one would volunteer for this.*

■ ·■■ · ■■■·· ■■ ·· · ■■■■

Mitchell filed the arriving doctor's paperwork and noticed that every page was labelled 'TOP SECRET by Order of DOD'.

"I don't know who this Dod might be," he confided to Goldie over lunch, "but the man sure sounds important."

For her part Goldie didn't look impressed. It took big news to distract her from her plate. Like most confined to Saint Laurent, she took mealtime seriously.

Her head snapped up, however, when Mitchell added, "The Administrator seems terrified. I've never seen anything like it." He continued, "Anything Dod's men want is theirs, no questions asked and no pushback. Including the attendant's breakroom."

Neither knew what lay behind the breakroom door. The tiny space was off-limits to residents, but Goldie focussed on what mattered, gesturing, 'WHEN'.

"It's being emptied this afternoon. You want to watch?"

Grim-faced soldiers carried everything out—a pair of mismatched couches, a battered coffee table, and a filthy, oversized ceramic ashtray—then thoroughly scrubbed the place and painted it a depressingly clinical beige.

'THIS NOT GOOD' Goldie didn't mince words.

"You can say that again," Mitchell agreed before heading to the Administrator's office, where a distinguished-looking man in a spotless lab-coat stood at the door, clearly waiting. "Yes?" Mitchell asked, pausing.

"I am expecting a delivery," the man announced. "I was told Mitchell could see to everything?"

"I'm Mitchell. What can I do for you?"

Taken aback by the statement, the man gathered his thoughts and answered politely, "Would you please make sure my equipment is placed in the new surgery."

Not having heard anything about a surgery, but figuring the man meant the newly remodelled breakroom, Mitchell said, "Yes, doctor." He guessed at the title but, seeing the man stand even taller, knew the guess was right. "Who's it from and when's it due to arrive?" Pen ready, the teen dutifully made notes.

"The Department of Defence will be making the delivery. Tomorrow. I have been assured of arrival before noon."

Fifteen crated boxes of varying sizes did indeed arrive the next day before noon. It seemed like every resident of the Louis Saint Laurent Institute for Crippled Children watched.

Word of the 'surgery' had spread like the hottest gossip, mostly because Mitchell told everyone. He sat front and centre as the unloading took place. Goldie parked right beside him. She even clapped when Mitchell signed for the crates.

The surgery didn't have enough room for much of an audience, so it fell to Mitchell to supervise from the door as two soldiers unpacked enough medical equipment to fill a hospital. All of it brand new…and nothing at the Louis Saint Laurent Institute was ever new.

It took days for the surgery to open, long days that had every resident openly curious. Every resident except Mitchell. Since the government documented everything, and one teenage resident filed all Institute's paperwork, he knew everything…and was all too happy to talk about it. With Goldie at least.

"There's a new treatment. Something 'ground-breaking'," Mitchell hurried to add. "They say it had 'remarkable' results on mice and they want to move to human testing."

His friend frowned at that. She didn't move for a long while, thinking, then said, "WE. ARE. EXPERIMENTS."

"Did you not hear 'Remarkable'," he stressed the word. "And no, I don't know what that means," Mitchell said before she could. "Look around. Any improvement is a miracle around here."

"EXPERIMENTS. NEED. TESTS. THAT. MEANS. A. CONTROL. GROUP."

Though neither were scientists, they'd been poked and prodded all their lives. They listened and learned the lingo. Both knew that someone always got the placebo.

"WHO. GETS. LEFT. OUT?" Goldie asked.

For once in his life Mitchell found he had nothing to say.

■ ·■"■ · ■■·-·"■ ·--·"■■■ ■

"Are we ready?"

Looking up from his meticulous work, Dr. Lourdes needed a moment to parse the general's meaning. "Everything appears in order," he confirmed before adding, "I need only review my notes, complete several final reports, and prepare the doses. It should take but a few days."

"I want to start today," General Bradley sounded like a disappointed toddler. The impression intensified as he bargained, "Can we not speed this up? Get that crippled kid, what's his name, to help with the paperwork. He seems able enough…for simple tasks."

INSTITUTING A CYCLE OF VIOLENCE

Musing, Claudio Mique-Alejandro Lourdes eventually nodded. "I suppose some carefully supervised assistance would not go amiss."

"So, what are we talking? Give me a timeline."

"Assuming all goes to plan…we can begin the day after tomorrow. Early." Dr. Lourdes paused, "How, exactly, are the injections to proceed?"

The general smiled, "Everything's arranged. The staff will start the day the same as usual but load our subjects onto gurneys rather than start their normal morning routines. They'll be wheeled in here so you can do your thing."

"You do understand that this course of treatment is unprecedented and unpredictable? It requires two separate procedures. The initial stage involves inserting a large-bore needle directly into the spinal column in order to introduce the compound. A complex injection, it will be both slow and painful."

Waving that concern aside, General Bradley said, "The disabled live in pain every day."

"As you say," came the unconvinced agreement. "In that case, I should be able to finish the first stage before noon. The second dose is the trigger. That, at least, should prove a simple process. We mix it in with their midday meal. Once administered, we should see results almost immediately. Though only God above knows what those will be."

"World-changing, doc," a bone-shaking back-slap accompanied the jovial announcement. "What we're doing here will go down in the history books, mark my words."

■ ▪ ▪■ ▪ ▪■■▪▪▪▪■ ▪▪▪■▪■■

Eliminating the placebos proved easy…once Mitchell discovered how to decode the doctor's remarkably bad handwriting.

St. Laurent's overworked staff had long ago come to trust him with complex tasks. Dr. Lourdes, on finding himself pulled a hundred different ways, had 'borrowed' Mitchell for "A straightforward exercise."

Filling the syringes, the doctor assured, was simple. "Merely load forty-six needles from the yellow-topped bottle and forty-six from the red-topped. Be sure to mark each either 'Y' and 'R', depending. Understand?"

Mitchell's confirming nod sent the man scurrying off on other, more important duties and left the teen free to search out Goldie. He offered a terse, "We got work to do," before leading the way back to the empty surgery.

"Which do you think is the placebo?" Mitchell asked, staring at the bottles sitting on the worktable besides waiting boxes of syringes.

Without hesitation Goldie pointed to one bottle then, grinning, spelled out 'LABEL' on her board.

Sure enough, the yellow-topped bottle had 'Placebo' written on its front. "That makes this the good stuff, then," Mitchell reached for a red-topped bottle, its label featured a string of sloppily scrawled chemical compounds. "What say we fill them all from here?" Goldie's nod was so emphatic that her wheelchair rocked.

When the pair were done, Mitchell carefully wrote 'R' on one half and 'Y' on the other exactly as instructed.

Locking the surgery, he said, "Well, there's our good deed done for the day."

Judging by the enormous smile splitting Goldie's face, she agreed.

INSTITUTING A CYCLE OF VIOLENCE

■ ■■ ■ ■■ ■ ■■ ■ ■ ■■ ■■

"The injections went smoothly," Dr. Lourdes reported when the increasingly anxious general checked in just before lunch the next morning.

"Good. Then we can enact phase two. Won't be long now, doctor. All our work, all our risks. It's pay-off time, you'll see."

"I, too, hope we succeed. After everything…to fail now would truly be devastating."

Despite his ample frame, General Bradley had no room in him for doubt. He believed the best, of himself and his future. "We'll crack it, never you worry. There's nothing a bit of can-do American spirit can't do."

■ ■■ ■ ■■ ■ ■■ ■ ■ ■■ ■■

Lunchtime arrived and with it came a special treat: milkshakes.

Mitchell had finished half of his, in one gloriously brain-freezing slurp, before he noticed Goldie's hesitant frown. She sipped again, taking the daintiest pull from her straw and moving the beverage around in her mouth before pointing, 'TASTE. FUNNY?'

Fighting a surging ice-cream headache, Mitchell didn't feel up to commenting. In that he wasn't alone. All around the Saint Laurent cafeteria residents were similarly suffering.

Groans echoed. Moans followed. Someone vomited and that started still others. A scream, it took Mitchell a long moment to realize it came from his own throat.

Panicking, he looked across at Goldie. She had blood dripping from her nose. And not a slow trickle either. Bright red fluid gushed like a waterfall. Her eyes were wide, and she clawed at her tray, trying to point. Unfortunately, as with the rest of the Institute's residents, she no longer had control over her body.

For the first and only time in his life Mitchell Connors felt grateful that his friend was non-verbal. It meant he didn't have to hear Goldie scream for help as she died.

■ ·■■ · ■■·· ■■ ··· ■■■ ■

Claudio Mique-Alejandro Lourdes looked on in horror. Standing frozen as all the children suffered and, one by one, died, he couldn't stop whispering, "What have we done?"

Deep in his heart, however, Dr. Lourdes knew. *The boy! He didn't use the placebo.* With no control group their experiment was a failure.

Watching, helpless, as the Juice wrought changes on ninety-two young bodies, overwriting their very beings down to the cellular level. The children suffered as genes shifted, slowly and painfully, before being reformed even more painfully—or, rather, trying to reform and failing.

General Bradley drifted into the cafeteria and stopped to stare at the scene. Recognizing a catastrophe in the making, he gathered his wits and began distancing himself from the colossal failure. Eyes hard he said, "Looks like your experiment took an unfortunate turn, doc."

"Unfortunate? Unfortunate! We have a room full of dying children!"

"No, Lourdes. You have a room full of…" unwilling to give voice to the truth, the general finished, "test subjects." Warming to the theme, he continued, "Each awaiting autopsy. Imagine what the American government will learn when you cut them open?"

INSTITUTING A CYCLE OF VIOLENCE

The room stank of spilled milkshakes and death. Claudio opened his mouth to deny that but, unable to help himself, began considering the possibilities. Then remembered: Ninety-eight percent.

A weak cough cut through the eerie quiet. It didn't come from him or the general.

Amidst the broken corpses, a resident stirred.

"It worked," the general whispered. "One of them survived. Now the billion-dollar question: Did they gain superpowers?"

■ ·■ ■ · ■ ■·· ■ ■ · · · ■ ■ ■ ■

Mitchell opened his eyes to find two intense figures leaning way too close. "What?"

"How do you feel?" the doctor demanded, reaching forward to examine the teen.

"Goldie?!"

"I'm sorry, son. She's gone," a uniformed man said. He didn't sound sorry. "They're all gone. Off to their just rewards."

It took Mitchell a long minute to realize the three were alone. His friends' bodies had already been moved. Sentimentality doesn't exist in institutions like Saint Laurent, he remembered.

Then it hit him. "You did this!" Anger unlike anything the teen had ever felt surged through him. "You played on our hope and used it to take advantage of us."

"We did our duty. America needs super-powered soldiers and that meant taking risks. None of us enjoyed it. We're not monsters."

Mitchell shook his head at the answer. "Risks? What risks? Me and my friends were experimented on. You just…watched." Bursting with hurt, guilt, and loss the teen felt his lungs gain strength. He didn't yell. He didn't have to. His voice conveyed his rage, words striking literal blows. "Almost a hundred dead kids and you think it's over? That you can just walk away, write a report, and get another fancy ribbon?"

Both general and doctor were knocked back. "The procedure works," Dr. Lourdes whispered.

Being more practical-minded General Bradley drew his sidearm, aimed it two-handed, and shouted, "Stay back!"

Gunshots echoed, deafening in the cafeteria. None of the bullets reached the teen.

Mitchell stopped them with his voice, announcing, "You two may not believe yourselves monsters…BUT YOU CREATED ONE!" He didn't know how he did it. His body remained unchanged, far from the muscled hero of story, still needing his wheelchair to move.

But now power surged through him. Talking had literally become his superpower and, having a lot to say, he smiled. There was none of his usual warmth in the expression. It barely looked human.

What happened next involved blood and pain and eighteen long years of being made to feel less.

One abandoned teen brought justice to the murderers of his friends—ninety-one disabled children—who died in fear and confusion; all while the people meant to protect and heal them took careful notes.

The Louis Saint Laurent Institute Massacre marked the birth of a new era for the world…one where the crippled fought back.

THINKING INSIDE *THE BOX*

BY HOLLY SCHOFIELD

CN: Off-screen death

The problem with cubicle farms is the lack of privacy. I flicked through pages on my screen while Mother Load's unmistakable voice rasped from the aisle a few cubes away. "How're the new admin staffers getting on? How's the neurodivergent one?"

I pricked up my ears. Just in the figurative sense—I don't have that particular superpower. She must be talking to Frisson, the nasty recruiting manager. He'd had it in for me since I'd aced the job interview, scoring better than the other two new employees despite his predictions.

Sure enough, Frisson gave his distinctive snort. "They're all terrible. And Donna Chow is worse than the other two."

THINKING *INSIDE* THE BOX

I began to bristle. Not like Porcupine Man or anything, but because it was so untrue. I was good at my job—excellent at it, in fact, as Frisson's own rigorous testing had shown. My particular flair for seeing patterns and being ultra-focused made me perfect to fill out all the forms WhistleClean needed to stay in business: hazmat suits orders, environmental assessment applications, tax refund forms for taxes paid on refunded taxes (the Canadian government is about as efficient as a vacuum cleaner on the Moon), anything and everything. I'd been deep in the system, typing at top speed, until this interruption sent my anxiety levels soaring.

MagNolia stuck her head around the cubicle corner. "Stay calm," she mouthed.

"You've got paperclips stuck to your face again," I whispered back. Her particular flair, a magnetic personality (iron and nickel, mainly), had its drawbacks.

"Whups, thanks for being blunt!"

I knew she meant it. She got me, unlike most neurotypicals.

Josh swivelled around from his cube behind me. "Hey, you can handle this!" He winked with his X-ray eyeball and gave me a thumbs up, just as Mother Load strode into view at the far end of the aisle. In my two weeks on the job, I'd only been face-to-face with her once, the day I was hired. I was pretty sure my heart had trembled when she'd swirled her cape and shaken my hand.

I hadn't wanted to wash it ever again (my hand, I mean) but I had. But only because I'd ridden the LRT home that day (the Light Rapid Transit system, I mean, not the Large Rainproof Troglodyte although sometimes I did opt to get carried places by him in a downpour, nice and dry in his huge fist). Various oozing body parts had littered my train car; the super-villain Berserker

Clown had been pretty active . Edmonton had become a harsher place since the solar flare had changed everything five years ago.

Mother Load and Frisson were coming closer. I tightened my ponytail. Our probation period ended today. Without our paycheques, the three of us would lose everything. Maybe I wouldn't have to say anything; my awful social skills kept costing me jobs—I'd been fired from seven jobs already this year, just for stating the obvious. I bent down to tighten my shoelaces.

I ran through a mental litany of my super-skills, while trying to lower my pulse rate. Like ten percent of North Americans, the solar flare had given me a superpower, enhancing what I was already good at. I couldn't lift the CN Tower or drink Niagara Falls dry, but I had truly impressive detail-finding skills. Frisson's recruiting test (I shuddered in recollection) had simply confirmed that.

Deep breaths, I told myself. *And remember not to be so literal and pedantic with anything they say.*

Frisson's shiny oxfords appeared on the grey carpet next to my shoes, followed by Mother Load's scarlet booties.

"What're you at, then?" Mother Load's Newfoundland accent was as thick as the warmth in her voice. People said she was too nice to be CEO-and-founder, and too short and elderly and ugly, but I thought she was more awesome than anyone I'd ever met, even Totally Awesome Man. Her particular flair was pollution detection using her marvellously large nose. What could be better than cleaning up the world?

"Napping, are you?" Frisson gloated.

I bumped my head on the underside of the desk, then straightened. "Mother Load," I squeaked.

Her salt-and-pepper brush cut and her scarlet costume exactly matched the poster of her I'd hung on my cubicle wall. And my living room wall. And my bicycle handlebars.

Frisson's narrow face and pinched forehead spoiled the moment. How could I prove my worth?

"Ma'am?" I twisted in my seat. "Would you like to see my accomplishments so far today?" I waved at the 42 tabs currently open on my monitor, my hand wobbling like The Nervous Tick's.

"The timestamps are on the d-d-documents," I stuttered. "I got them all done with time to spare, on time, in a timely way." I clamped my mouth shut firmly. I wanted to add that I'd been working on combining four forms into a single more effective one just now by my own initiative, but I was afraid I'd babble more.

Frisson peered at the timestamps. "What have you been doing the past hour? Playing Minesweeper?" He crossed his arms over his grey suit. "Madam Load, lazy people do not belong at WhistleClean. She has to go. I have a replacement in mind. A fine candidate named Sonya Herring."

"But I'm good at this!" I stood and faced him. My chair banged against the cubicle wall.

"Ms. Chow should be let go, Ma'am. Shouting like this is unacceptable. Fire the other two as well since they aren't any better either."

Mother Load held up a hand. "Oh, me nerves. Frisson, I trust your judgement. MagNolia, Josh, you be off now. You there"—she glanced at my desk nameplate—"Donna, fill out three employee dismissal forms, there's a gal." I sat.

Obediently.

I was the only kid in kindergarten who coloured inside the lines.

My therapist said it wasn't just societal pressure to be a "good girl" but a generous heap of autism (and a dash of ADHD) as well.

So I follow rules and fill forms.

Day after day. Year after year.

Mostly.

As Josh and MagNolia mournfully headed for the elevator, and before I pulled up Form #387b-rev.4.5 (Termination of Junior Administrative Personnel), I typed "Sonya Herring" into my customized search engine, stabbing at the keyboard as Frisson droned on about my shortcomings and Mother Load shifted her feet, looking miserable.

I managed to tune them both out until I was sure of what I was finding. "Ma'am?"

"I'm so sorry, Donna. These things happen." Mother Load's flair graced her with the ability to sniff out toxic waste, and made WhistleClean a successful company, but I suspected she hated the managerial aspect that went with it.

"But… Ma'am?" The search showed that Sonya had attended Frisson's junior high school in Mississauga and that they'd both eaten at the same sushi place at West Edmonton Mall last week. And there was an eighty-seven percent overlap between Sonya and Frisson in everything from Facebook friends to genomic biomarkers to supermarket points. I squinted at the screen, teasing out the pattern.

"Ms. Chow doesn't even have the people skills to defend herself," Frisson said, his voice dripping scorn the way Nostril Man dripped mucus.

"I dunno, Frisson. Maybe she deserves a second chance." Mother Load smiled at me. Me!

I went mute. Couldn't say a word. Selective mutism was *not* my favourite neurodivergent superpower (even though it worked well for Gossip Girl). I waved my nameplate at my screen silently.

Mother Load squinted at it and shook her head. Maybe she needed glasses.

Frisson glanced at the Herring/Frisson chart I'd made and paled. He waved a hand in a complicated, majestic fashion.

My office chair scooted from underneath me and I was instantly on hands and knees in a silver three-foot by two-foot tunnel. That familiar, awful HVAC ducting above my cubicle.

I'd been teleported.

Again.

Frisson's flair enables him to teleport anything for short distances. Putting job candidates in an air-conditioning duct meant Frisson could easily separate quality recruits from losers, at least in his opinion. Make the candidate crawl through a forking tunnel and ask them forking difficult questions: "How many golf balls fit into a Shoppers Drug Mart?" "Who would win, in a fight between William Shatner and Trudeau?" And without even telling you which Trudeau! (I'd bet on Margaret and been right).

"What have you gone and done?" Mother Load's voice made my sheet metal prison ring.

"Just another hiring test. Second chance, like you said. If she passes, they all can stay."

I pressed against the cold wall, surprised to find I was still clutching my nameplate, hunting for words. "Ma'am? Sonya Herring is Frisson's second cousin. Her flair is knowing who will take a bribe. Frisson either took a bribe or succumbed to nepotism. Or both."

"Me nerves, me nerves! Frisson, is that true?"

I ignored Frisson's impassioned defence and crawled to the first junction, a few metres away. Red laser beams criss-crossed the tunnel just ahead, threatening to fry me if I went further. On the wall, the embedded screen Frisson had teleported there glowed: "Which weighs more, a pound of feathers or a pound of gold?" To turn off the laser beams, I only had to enter a correct answer and hit "Submit". If I got four questions right, Frisson would teleport me out.

I relaxed, like I always do when a procedure becomes clear and social interaction isn't required.

Mother Load's voice made the tunnel vibrate. "Frisson, I may not be able to sniff out human corruption but this time I smell a rat! You're fired!"

"Uh, Ma'am," I ventured. "Can Frisson let me out of here first?"

"Not a chance!" Frisson's evil cackle died away and I heard elevator buttons ding.

Mother Load called up to me, "A touch too late for that, I'm some sorry. You'll just have to wait a tick. I'm having my best security guard meet up with Frisson downstairs and force him to transport ya out." Her voice dropped as she mumbled instructions into her Bluetooth, then rose again: "Or I s'pose you could answer the interview questions?"

"Sure, that's okay then, it's all good." I started to type "the same" into the screen's answer field. Above my hovering finger, the word pattern caught my eye.

Frisson had changed the question.

My heart hammered against my ribs like Ballpeen Kid in a shopping cart.

THINKING *INSIDE* THE BOX

The question now read, "Which weighs more: a kilo of feathers in Petawawa, or a kilo of gold on the moon?"

I ran definitions of mass through my head as best as I could remember from high school then hesitantly typed in "Feathers".

The light flashed green, pointing left, and I realized I'd bitten my lip enough to bleed.

The laser beams turned off and I crawled through to the next junction, catching my suit pants several times on protruding screw points. No matter—if I didn't get out of this ceiling prison, I wouldn't need my pants anyway. I'd be pretty much unemployable and I'd go back to wearing a polyester uniform. The only forms I'd be filling out would involve extra orders of fries and I always spilled those (the fries, not the forms).

"Hope you're all right in there," Mother Load's voice rang loud and clear. From the sound of her voice, she seemed to be following along below me. "I'm pondering it. I think this here calls for thinking outside the box."

Thinking *inside* the box was what I was good at. Everyone said so. And this sure was a box. "Ma'am? Can you possibly open a hatch? Or cut a hole?"

"Cut through good ducting? Not terrible green now, in'nt? Let's wait just a bit. Frisson teleported you up there and he can bloody well teleport you out. I've given Stomping Tom strict instructions regarding Frisson. Oh, and I'm sittin' here at your desk. You've done a right big amount of work here, me gal. I can't make head or tail of these forms, meself."

I mused all that over as I crawled. Stomping Tom the security guard wasn't known for following instructions. I came to the next junction. "What makes waves in a Delta?" I thought for a minute.

The ocean? But not exactly in a delta. An EEG, maybe, recording delta waves? But why a capital D? I remembered a long-ago trip to Vancouver Island that left from a region called Delta and hesitantly entered, "A ferry docking at Tsawwassen", hoping I'd spelled it right. Green light. The angry laser beams up ahead turned off. Whew.

I crawled along turning right, head scraping the ceiling, clutching my silly name plate like a talisman of my doom. Even if I got out of here alive, why would Mother Load continue to employ awkward, anxious me? And if she did, how long could I stand filling out boring forms day after day? My bleak future stretched ahead of me like so much A/C ducting. Only the presence of MagNolia and Josh made working here bearable. But they despaired about their boring jobs too.

Next junction. More angry red lasers. "How many frisbees would be floating in the air on a summer Saturday at 6 p.m. EST in central Saskatchewan? Your answer must be correct to the nearest hundred."

"Ma'am? Can you call up a search engine and see how many city parks there are in Regina?"

"Includin' the provincial legislature grounds?" I could hear the click of my keyboard as she pecked away at it. Three minutes later (two-and-a-half more minutes than it would have taken me) she called up a figure.

"Thanks!" I called back and factored it into my mental back-of-the-envelope calculation. The lasers faded and the green light glowed as nicely as Peppermint Grandpa had that time I'd carried his Nanaimo bar and soy latte over to his table at Second Cup.

I arrived at the next corner. A short distance ahead: a hatch! The way out! Unfortunately, it lay just past the final set of lasers and the final question: "Which horse will win the Fall Classic at Northlands Park tomorrow?"

The question sounded a bit desperate. I could see the pattern in my mind's eye, like the weaving in a blanket. A horse blanket. Frisson must have a gambling addiction and taken bribes from Sonya Herring so he could place bets at the track! I shook my head then shook it again. I needed to focus. If there were dozens of horses racing in the Classic, eight horses per race, and I didn't know any of their names, my chance of getting it right were, well, less than the chance that the Leafs would win the Cup.

The Grey Cup.

I was doomed. And so were the only friends I'd ever made my entire life.

"You'll have to cut open the ducting," I called. "I'm stuck on the final question." I read it aloud to Mother Load.

It sounded even worse the second time.

"Oh. Tough one, inn't? The custodian is fetching a pair of tin snips but I'm truly not knowin' where you're at." A banging noise right below me. "There, love, I'm standing on your desk, whacking away on the ceiling with a broom handle. Can you hear it?"

The thump was steady and close, which didn't make sense since I should be far away from my desk by now, but I couldn't think straight; I was gasping for breath and sweating.

The question on the screen flickered, replaced by an image of crimp-mouthed Frisson, showing sharp teeth. "That's right, Donna, you're running out of air. And I've raised the temperature a few degrees. Enjoy." He laughed maniacally and the screen went dark.

"Hang in there, me gal. Help is on its way. Not more than half an hour or so. And I've got my staff looking into all of Frisson's hires." Mother Load's voice was as strong and clear as ever.

Huh.

Whether she was standing, sitting at my desk, or standing on top of it, her voice had the same volume, even though I'd crawled at least twenty metres. I drew a map in my mind: by now I should be above Jasper Avenue's lunch-hour traffic.

Also, how come there wasn't any air in an air-conditioning duct?

The puzzle pieces fell into place.

This had to be a hallucination. Frisson wasn't a teleporter, he was a *mind controller*. It was all symbolic: the ducting, the maze, the junctions, even the nameplate in my hand. Minor miraging must be his only superpower; otherwise he'd have transported his chosen horse right over the finish line or moved the closest CIBC's vault contents to his wallet.

All I had to do was overcome his mirage. Easy peasy.

I closed my eyes and pictured the metal ducting turning to thin plastic. My hand hurt as I imagined the nameplate turning into a chisel. I opened my eyes and pounded my chisel on the now-white, now-plastic floor in front of me, feeling my throat close in.

One chip and then another, then a wide swath of plastic let loose below me.

A crackling noise and grey carpet rushed up to meet me.

I may have shouted.

A relieved chuckle and the scritchy-scratchy sound of a hand running over a buzzcut. I'd appeared at the feet of Mother Load.

She cleared her throat, cape fluttering, arms akimbo. "Well, Donna, this inn't so terrible awful, now is it. All's well that ends, me daddy always—hang on." She answered her beeping Bluetooth. "Let me hit speakerphone." She touched a button and caught my eye. "Stomping Tom has cornered Frisson, down in the parkade."

"Tell Tom that Frisson's a miragic, not a teleporter," I said hastily. "He's limited in the visions he forces on you, HVAC ducting and whatnot. I was on the floor of my cubicle the whole time. All he did was make me believe that I was up in the ducting—and make you believe it too, Ma'am. But there's a way to fight it. If you are strong enough and have the ability to see patterns"—I paused, filled with pride—"you can overcome his visions by superimposing your own pattern of reality."

Mother Load's eyebrows rose higher and higher as she conveyed the message.

Through the speaker, Frisson ordered Stomping Tom to stop in his tracks.

A gruff voice told *him* to stop in *his* tracks.

"I'll teleport you, Stomping Tom! To the moon! Or to Mars!"

"Hands up, Frisson! That's my last warning!" The gruff voice got gruffer.

There was a moment's silence. I bit my sore lip. If I was wrong about things, Stomping Tom was on his way somewhere unpleasant.

Frisson swore.

Stomping Tom laughed. Gruffly, of course. "Hey, buddy, did I mention my side-flair is a total lack of imagination? If you're trying to insert one of your hallucinations in my massive head, it's not working."

Frisson swore again, this time in the other official language. "That's it! You got it coming now, buddy!" Even gruffer.

Mother Load shouted, "Tom! Don't you be doin' that!"

There was a noisy squelch. Not like an electronic sort of squelch, but like a massive boot coming down on bubble wrap. Frisson was about to be subjected to a few hours of listening to pop-pop-popPOP-pop as Stomping Tom did his thing. Like I said, Stomping Tom wasn't known for following instructions well. Like I also said, it's a less kind, less gentle world nowadays.

Mother Load sighed. "Can't win 'em all, now can we." She clapped me on the shoulder. "Thanks, me love, for figuring everythin' out. I do have me regrets that I completely misjudged that slieveen, Frisson."

I lifted my head and nodded.

Her Bluetooth pipped again. Still on speakerphone, we listened to her VP report their investigations. And we winced at the same time.

Mother Load threw up her hands. "Twelve employees hired last year are Frisson's relatives? Including most of my task force? Yes, by the Lord's own sweet tears, fire them. Fire them all!" She closed the connection with a firm tap of her finger then cocked her head at me and held out a hand. "There's someone else I misjudged."

"Ma'am?"

"How'd ya like to find patterns in sewage outlets and city rivers? I think ya'd be good at it. And I happen to have me some recent openings in the pollution sleuthing task force."

I squinted, picturing the pattern of my future: a dream come true!

I squared my shoulders. "I can't do that, Ma'am." I'd come to like my cubicle life, for two simple reasons: one of them soldiering on in the cubicle beside me and one who always had my back.

Mother Load sputtered like Frothy Boy in a bubble bath. If I did stay on with WhistleClean, I'd have to let her know that sometimes it takes me a while to get my words out.

I held up a pleading hand, concentrating hard. "Not unless there's also room on the team for MagNolia and Josh. Maybe Mag could find rare earth metals in tailing ponds? And Josh could X-ray into collapsed buildings?"

Mother Load let air out through her nose and chuckled. "I think we can manage that, dear."

We beamed at each other. Not like Beam Me Up Scotty, but like we were happy.

Which we were.

MASKING UP

BY ERIN ROCKFORT

CN: Non-graphic violence, light body horror

First things first: being a superhero kicks ass. Literally and metaphorically.

How else can you make meaningful change, help the people in your community? And what better way to make friends? With heroes, you've got built-in similarities: powers, separation from the world, and, of course, a strong sense of justice.

You see, I'd never been good at socializing, even before I gained the ability to generate force fields. As a kid, I enforced the rules for the others. I'd tell them off for playing with the light switch, or running when they weren't supposed to. Lawful Good, you might call me, and it turns out, most people don't love that.

So I became Paladin: the Shield of Justice. Putting on the mask felt like coming home. For the first time, I had a set of absolute rules I could follow; I could step into being Paladin and forget my awkward, unlikeable civilian self behind. I could relax into being a hero, into doing the right thing, as predetermined by heroes who had come before.

But I digress; this story isn't about me. After all, who wants to hear about a mid-tier autistic hero who mostly spends her time saving cats from trees?

This story is about her — about Siren.

If you're here, you know her, of course. She appeared like the sun through the world's smog, using her powers to defeat the mega-billionaires turning their wealth towards super-villainy. She ushered in the Age of Heroes, as they call it, when supers rose to prominence and the world changed forever.

As a teenager, I watched her change the world. Her posters plastered my room: silver costume, blonde hair streaming behind her, luminescent wings propelling her into the sky. She watched over my every awkward social stumbling, my every failed attempt at connecting. I even ran a fan page for her on social media.

When my powers emerged, I wanted nothing more than to follow in her footsteps.

So you can understand why I would attend an event labelled as a "Hero's Gala," sponsored by Siren and Dynamico, the city's leading corporation. I received the email in my Paladin inbox, and the details checked out; somehow, I'd gained an invite. My dreams had never extended as far as meeting Siren in the flesh, as a peer rather than a fan. If I'd had her powers, I would have glowed in excitement at the thought.

That night, I suited up as usual. An EVA foam breastplate and a Dynamico thermoplastic helmet, skills learned from my cosplay days, made up my costume; my powers did the actual work of keeping me safe. I hoped the suit would pass scrutiny in a brightly-lit room full of professionals.

The Gala had been advertised as occurring at City Hall, which bustled with activity when I arrived, full of all manner of local heroes. I picked my way inside, concentrating hard to make sure I didn't whack into any of them; my dyspraxia and general lack of proprioception had gotten me in trouble before. I showed my invitation, and the workers waved me into the atrium, where I stopped in my tracks.

Ahead of me stood a room full of other superheroes, ones I had only ever seen on the news: Crimson Hammer, Joust, Ethereal Phoenix, and, in the middle, Siren, there in the flesh. She nearly didn't look real, all shining hair and sparkling costume.

Once the shock wore off, excitement buzzed through me. I shook my hands back and forth, stimming to use some of the energy, before stepping further in. Under my mask, I chewed rigorously on my tongue.

Glass clinked, and the conversation in the room ceased as the assembled heroes turned to the source of the noise. I recognized the mayor, standing next to Siren at a raised podium.

"Welcome, heroes!" the mayor greeted, smiling widely. "I am honoured to welcome you all tonight, and to be standing amongst you. Or, as 'amongst' as I can — I still can't fly!"

This elicited a round of laughter from the room. I kept silent, not sure that I understood the joke.

"This night is to celebrate the good that you do for this city, so please, eat, mingle, enjoy yourselves. And thank you, from the bottom of my heart."

The room applauded him, and I followed suit, while already making my way over to the before-mentioned food. As I crossed the room, I kept my eyes open for anyone I might recognize from the circuit. Mostly, I hoped I might find someone I could attach myself to for the night.

I inspected the spread, finding it to be respectable. A proper way to honour the city's heroes would be a real dinner, in my opinion, but I couldn't find fault with the steaming breaded shrimp, the prosciutto-wrapped fruit, or the potstickers. They even had dessert, little piles of profiteroles and cannolis.

While considering whether or not the prosciutto would be texturally upsetting, I bumped into someone from behind.

"Oh, I'm so —" I began, only to stutter to a stop. I'd walked into none other than Siren, *the* Siren. I said something eloquent like, "Uh buh duh?"

Siren smiled behind her silvery mask. "I don't think we've met before. I'm Siren."

"I know," I blurted, "I'm a huge fan. I mean. Uh. That's probably weird, right? Uh —"

"Relax, kid," she said, laughing. "What's your name?"

"Kate — uh. Paladin, I mean." I tried for a smile.

Either Siren didn't notice my difficulty and my desire to sink into my boots, or had the decency not to acknowledge it. "I don't think I've seen you around," she said. "What's your specialty?"

"Uh, a bit of everything, I guess," I said haltingly. "Small-time stuff, mostly. I make shields."

Siren smiled. She seemed to shine out of her pores, transfixing me. It wasn't even one of her powers. "Come with me, Paladin. I'd like you to meet some people."

I followed her, rehearsing introductions in my head. Of course, when she led me to a group of A-list heroes, living legends in their own right, and introduced me, all I could say was "Ahh?" My brain shorted out; I didn't have a script for this.

They all nodded politely at me, and then greeted Siren like an old friend, welcoming her to the group. I faded into the background, not unhappily. That way, I couldn't embarrass myself any further. They had better things to do than talk to the newbie; I glowed just to feel included in the group.

"Crime has been up this quarter," noted one hero, Vindicator, in a deep voice.

"Crime's always up," responded another, Criss Cross. "How else are we meant to stay busy?"

Ethereal Phoenix hit him with a delicate gloved hand and chided, "You shouldn't say things like that." She looked at me pointedly.

"Oh, don't worry about me," I blurted out. "I get it. Crime doesn't sleep, right? The more heroes, the more villains emerge, and on and on. Not to say that you're — that we're — causing a crime wave. Obviously."

If I could have withered into a puddle, I would have. The looks I received in return seemed perplexed, amused. These weren't unusual looks, of course, but I could have lived without ever seeing them on the faces of my literal heroes.

MASKING UP

Before I could hear their response, though, an alarm went off, complete with flashing light. I glanced at Siren, who appeared alert, but not concerned. She leaned towards me, and said in a confidential whisper, "Someone's up to no good. Figures, eh? No rest for the wicked."

I nodded, though truthfully, I didn't know how much superheroing she still performed. Still, she waved down the mayor, and said, "Don't worry, Mr Mayor. I've got this one." He appeared visibly relieved that she had taken the responsibility of dealing with the crisis off his plate.

Then, she turned to me. "Want to come?"

"What?"

"You know, see how the vets get things done. Maybe you'll teach us a few things, too." She smiled a thousand-watt smile.

All I could do was nod vaguely again, and chew my tongue. The night had been surreal already, but a chance to work directly with Siren? As scary as it seemed, I couldn't pass it up.

In the end, she also recruited Vindicator, who seemed eager to exit the party. He wore his customary dark armour, visor concealing any identifying features. I followed their steps, attempting to match their pace exactly. When we reached the street, Vindicator let me climb on the back of his motorcycle, and Siren's shiny, chitinous wings emerged from her back; she took to the sky, and we followed on the bike.

The alarm had apparently been related to a break-in at a warehouse just outside of the downtown core. You know how all cities have a warehouse district in case of superhero fights? Yeah. In any case, it seemed deserted; no obvious sign of crime.

"So, what's the plan?" I whispered, stepping off of the bike as Siren alighted beside us.

She and Vindicator exchanged a glance, and then she said, "I'll scan the perimeter. Vin, take Paladin through the back. Make sure she doesn't get hurt."

I followed Vindicator around the warehouse, once again trying to copy his moves. I worked best with instruction; when my powers first emerged, I'd read a ton of articles and blogs about How To Be A Hero before I could even think about going out for the first time.

As we approached the back door, a high, keening noise came from the west. Vindicator held up a hand.

"I will investigate this," he said firmly. "Scout into the warehouse. Do not engage the hostiles."

And like that, I stood alone before the door. I shuddered, unhappy, but unwilling to disobey a direct order. My nerves lit up like a Christmas tree as I pushed the door open, wincing when it creaked.

I stepped into the warehouse, hyper-aware of every noise I made: my footsteps on the concrete, my breath in the enclosed space. Around me, shelves piled high with boxes hid me from the interior, as well as anyone else who might be present.

Low, incomprehensible voices murmured further in, echoing off the walls. I crept forward, all my focus on controlling my motor functions. Heel-toe, heel-toe, elbows in, breath shallow. I had been told to scout, and damn it if I wouldn't follow those instructions.

Finally, I peeked around a shelf and caught sight of the intruders. There were three individuals, all in costume, apparently arguing with each other. After a moment, I realized that I recognized them: Glorious Gloom, in their shroud of darkness; the Quantum Spider, four spindly arms gesticulating around her; and a figure that, last I heard, was calling himself Mr. Pink Wasp.

I knew them all to be B-tier villains at best. Small-time crime, minor acts of mischief, only those activities that would put them on that radar of, well, me. And, clearly, despite scuffling with them all on previous occasions, I'd never put them away in any meaningful sense.

Next, I noticed what they had in their hands: cans of gasoline, the floor around them gleaming slickly.

Shocked, I stepped forward, trying to get a better look. Of course, in doing so, I misjudged the distance between myself and one of the shelves. Goddamn dyspraxia! The contents crashed to the floor with a tremendous sound. My hands flew to my ears to cover them.

The noise obviously drew the attention of the villains. For a moment, we stood in silence, staring at each other. Finally, Mr. Pink Wasp said, "Paladin, is that you?"

"Uh. Yeah." I waved, then cringed. "Hey Wasp. Still Wasp, right?"

"Yep," Wasp replied, just about as awkward as I felt.

Here's the thing about Wasp that I didn't mention: he and I actually went to school together. No, I won't tell you his real name. Actually, to be honest, I don't know his current civilian name; surely he no longer goes by the deadname I knew him as. Either way, though, it's just common courtesy. You never out someone without their permission.

"Come out of there," Quantum Spider said, her whispery voice still carrying in the echoing warehouse.

I did as instructed, stepping carefully into the open space where they stood. I could only hope that Siren and Vindicator wouldn't know how badly I'd screwed up.

"What are you doing here?" Wasp asked, a nervous edge to his voice.

"I'm…here to stop you?" I cleared my throat, then tried again, "Definitely here to stop you."

Glorious Gloom laughed. "Really? You seem at a disadvantage, friend."

"I'm not alone," I hedged, warring between expectations of accuracy and secrecy. "I think it'd be best if you all got out of here."

Quantum Spider blinked her four eyes at me. "Go home, Paladin," she said. "Forget about this."

"I won't! What are you even hoping to accomplish?"

Wasp stepped forward carefully, avoiding the gasoline on the floor. "Don't you know where we are?" When it became clear that I didn't, he said, "This is the Dynamico warehouse, where the company keeps its extra stock. Does anything seem out of place?"

My anxiety spiked; I didn't do well under pressure. Still, I looked around, and the answer came surprisingly quickly. When the boxes had fallen, their contents had spilled across the floor: weapons, armour, pseudo-military gear. Moreover, I identified symbols belonging to recognizable heroes and villains.

I felt woozy. "What is this?"

"Dynamico is double-dealing," Wasp said. "They're funding both sides, creating conflict."

"Why?"

Gloom spoke up. "Dynamico has its fingers in all sorts of pots. Development, property management, private contractors. Ever notice where most large-scale fights happen?"

"Low-income neighbourhoods," Quantum Spider answered for me. "Areas of the city no one will be too concerned about. We knock it down, they clean it up, and then they build it back better, more expensive."

I wanted to grab my head, tug on my hair. My teeth bit so deep on my tongue I tasted blood. "Okay, okay, well, that's — bad. Obviously. But arson won't solve that!"

"Maybe not," Wasp replied. "But it'll slow them down."

"But — but —" I could barely think. "Arson is still illegal, it's wrong, it's — it's bad for the environment! Probably!"

Wasp opened his mouth, but I never heard his reply. Siren burst through the ceiling, sending bits of plaster and insulation crashing to the floor. Vindicator stepped through a newly-formed hole in the side of the building. Both of them swiftly intercepted the action.

"Stop where you are," Siren commanded, hovering above the floor. "Good job, Paladin."

"Thanks?"

Wasp shot me an expression of unmistakable hurt, and I felt a gnawing, grasping sensation in my gut.

"Do not resist," Vindicator rumbled. "You are under arrest."

Quantum Spider leapt at him, long limbs grasping. Darkness seeped from Gloom. Wasp, meanwhile, pulled a lighter from his pocket. Before he could use it, Siren tackled him from the air, catching him in a headlock. I readied a shield, but it proved unnecessary; Vindicator had already caught the others in pieces of floor, manipulated to become cages.

I hated it. The emptiness in my gut grew until it consumed my being, and all I could do was shout, "Stop!"

"Is there a problem, Paladin?" Siren asked, a slight edge to her voice. She had wrestled the lighter away from Wasp, and it now lay in the middle of the floor.

"Y-yes!" I stuttered, trying not to sound childish. "These villains —they're bad, yes, but they have a reason! They were trying to prevent *worse* things!"

Vindicator's dark visor swung towards me. "What are you saying?"

I waved towards the broken boxes. "Dynamico is financing supervillains. They're trying to make our city worse so that they can control it! For their own gain!"

Siren and Vindicator exchanged a glance, and then she landed, leaving Wasp in a heap on the floor. "Paladin," she said, and I knew her tone. I had heard it a million times from teachers, parents, peers; it meant 'you don't get it' or 'you missed the point.' "Let's talk about this later. One on one."

"No," I said, looking at Wasp's unmoving form. "Let's talk about this right now."

Siren sighed, tossing her hair over her shoulder. "You want to be a hero? Okay, well, this is part of it; Dynamico keeps us going."

"Are you saying…you already knew?" I asked.

"Everyone knows, Paladin," Siren replied, her voice so gentle it made me want to throw something. "Consider yourself lucky; you're one of us, now."

Something broke deep inside of me. "But it's wrong," I tried weakly.

Siren shrugged. "Maybe," she said casually, like the word didn't pierce me like a knife. "But that's not up to us. We don't make the rules, we just follow them."

I took my mask off to shake my head, and then couldn't stop. My body felt like it had been taken over by bees, buzzing through my skin. I wanted to run away. I wanted to collapse in on myself. I wanted the time and space to figure out what to do about any of this. This hadn't been covered in the articles; what was I, a mid-tier autistic superhero, meant to do about it?

"Paladin," Wasp croaked, and the sound drew me from my stupor. "Get out of here."

Paladin. I *was* Paladin, and I had a duty: to this city, to him, to *myself*. I had to make this right if no one else could, or would. I stepped into the role of Paladin again, and I put the mask back on.

"Siren," I said, "Someone has to do the right thing. I'm sorry it couldn't be you."

"What —" Siren began, but I had already darted across the room, scooping up the lighter from where it had been dropped.

Before anyone could do anything to stop me, I had flicked it on.

"What are you doing, Paladin?" Siren demanded. "Are you really going to sacrifice everything?"

"To do the right thing?" I clarified. "Every time, Siren."

I dropped the lighter.

The fire whooshed through the gas on the floor. Siren shot up into the air, back out of the ceiling. Vindicator retreated too, flames licking at his heels. Within seconds, the warehouse had been engulfed. Had I not prepped my shield, I would have had a very nasty burn.

With an incandescent force field covering me head to toe, I stepped through the fire, following glowing trails to where Wasp lay. I had never used my shield in precisely this way, but I found him unharmed, staring wide-eyed around him. I helped him to his feet.

Together, we found Quantum Spider and Glorious Gloom, kept safe from the fire as well. When Vindicator fled, they had been freed from his contraption. I could feel the strain of maintaining the shield, but superheroes were my special interest; of course I had learned everything I could about my own powers.

Quantum Spider knew a safe route out of the warehouse, and within moments, we emerged into a deserted back alley. I looked back to see the building beginning to collapse, taking its evidence and all of my own hopes and dreams with it.

"Emergency vehicles will arrive soon," said Spider. "We should leave."

Wasp hesitated. "Come with us, Paladin. Help us out; we could do good together."

"Maybe," I agreed, "but I've got a lot of work ahead, I think. I want to do good, but I need to figure out what that is. I'm not sure that I know, anymore."

Wasp nodded, and gave me a sad smile. I felt heartened by the knowledge that maybe I didn't have to do all that relearning by myself.

"You'll know where to find us," said Quantum Spider, pressing my hand between three of hers.

Gloom shot me a thumbs-up, and then the three of them disappeared into the shadows.

So here we are. Our heroes have let us down. Siren has let us down. And I have no proof and no way forward. What do I do with that? What do any of us do with that? How can I continue to be the Shield of Justice when I'm not even sure what Justice means anymore?

I don't know. But, dear reader, I bring you this in the hope that we — all of us — can try to figure it out.

I think the world is going to need us to.

EDITORS AND CONTRIBUTORS

Learn more about the *Mighty* folks. If you enjoyed their stories, please consider following them on social media and/or finding out more about their other works.

ABOUT THE EDITORS

Emily Gillespie (she/they) is a mad and autistic author, disability activist, and professional daydreamer. Gillespie has a BA in Gender Equality and Social Justice an MA in Critical Disability Studies and a certificate in Creative Writing. They have volunteered and worked in the disability community as an activist, researcher, and facilitator for over ten years. Her writing explores themes of memory, identity and mental health journeys. They enjoy working in community spaces and examining individual and collective experiences. *Dancing with Ghosts* (Leaping Lion Books, 2017) is her first novel. Their poetry and short-stories can be found in several journals and anthologies.

She is currently drafting her second grant funded novel about the failures of the emergency mental health system. In her spare time Emily enjoys reading, walking, dancing, swimming and people watching in cafes throughout Toronto. Emily can be found curled up in her bed full of unicorn plushies dreaming of a more just and loving world for all marginalized and disabled folks.

Jennifer Lee Rossman (she/they) iis a queer, disabled, and autistic author and editor. They grew up befriending woodland creatures in the wilds around Oneonta, New York, but has since run away to the land of carousels and Rod Serling, also known as Binghamton.

Jennifer has over 50 short story publications, and is the coeditor of *Love & Bubbles* and *Space Opera Libretti* anthologies. You can find more of their work on their website http://jenniferleerossman. blogspot.com, and follow them on Twitter @JenLRossman.

ABOUT THE AUTHORS

Cait Gordon is an autistic, disabled, and queer Canadian writer of speculative fiction that celebrates diversity. She is the author of *Life in the 'Cosm, The Stealth Lovers*, and *Iris and the Crew Tear Through Space* (2023). Her short stories appear in *Alice Unbound: Beyond Wonderland, We Shall Be Monsters, Space Opera Libretti*, and *Stargazers: Microtales from the Cosmos*. Cait also founded The Spoonie Authors Network and joined Talia C. Johnson to co-edit the *Nothing Without Us* and *Nothing Without Us Too* anthologies, whose authors and protagonists are disabled, d/Deaf, Blind or visually impaired, neurodivergent, Spoonie, and/or they manage mental illness.

KS Palakovic is a health policy analyst for money, and a writer, singer, model, photographer, and rock climber for fun. For no money and questionable fun, she is also a queer, disabled, and neurodivergent woman.

Originally from Hamilton, Ontario—the city of waterfalls and steel—Katherine currently lives in Victoria, BC with her extremely fluffy cat and a growing collection of journals that no one is allowed to read.

Dave Lerner has known that he had ADHD for over fifty years, but only learned he's autistic about ten years ago.

He has written articles for Mythcreants.com and seanpcarlin.com, and some stories for private commissions, but this is his first professional fiction sale.

Polly Orr is a non-binary artist, activist and lover residing on the traditional unceded lands of the Hul'q'umi'num' speaking peoples. Their work has appeared in publications including *Anti-Lang, Filling Station,* and *Dodging the Rain,* as well as written into snowbanks after every blizzard.

Melissa Yuan-Innes loves everything from feminist fairy tales to Shaolin monks in space. She writes the critically-acclaimed Hope Sze medical thrillers, about a resident doctor bone deep in murder, as Melissa Yi. Melissa was diagnosed with normal tension glaucoma and looks forward to her superpowers. When she's not creating new worlds, Melissa hangs out with her family, including two rescue dogs. Find her on Facebook (Melissa Yi Yuan-Innes), Twitter @dr_sassy, and her website, http://www.melissayuaninnes.com/

Rowan Marci is an author of speculative fiction. She draws inspiration from the complex and beautiful experiences of being disabled, queer, and human. Rowan has worked for fourteen years as a mental health provider for youth. Her short stories have been published in anthologies by Quillkeepers Press and Northern Connecticut Writers Workshop. Rowan loves music she can dance to, snarky banter and adventures, real or imagined. She lives in Northwest Connecticut in the United States.

Shannon Barnsley is a writer, poet, and stroke survivor from New Hampshire, currently living in Brooklyn. She holds a degree in Creative Writing/Mythology & Religion from Hampshire College, land of llamas and LARPers. Since graduating, she has been found giving tours at an 18th century Shaker village museum, translating British English into American English for an independent publishing company, transcribing comic creator interviews for an intrepid con reporter, wandering in the woods, and tackling the epic journey that comes with being a real life mutant with multiple chronic illnesses. Her first book, *Beneath Blair Mountain*, was published by 1888 in Fall 2015.

E.D.E. Bell (she/her or e/em) loves fantasy fiction and enjoys blending classic and modern elements. A passionate vegan and earnest progressive, she feels strongly about issues related to equality and compassion.

Her works are quiet and queer and often explore conceptions of identity and community, including themes of friendship, family, and connection. She lives in Ferndale, Michigan, where she writes stories, revels in garlic and runs the creative side of her small press, Atthis Arts. You can follow eir adventures at edebell.com.

Beatrice Morgan's stories come life in a little village in England, surrounded by green hills. A chronically ill nature nerd, she is prone to waxing philosophical about the cosmological consequences of whale carcasses.

Emma Hardy is an Australian writer who is living and working in Las Vegas. Her writing has been published in *The Monthly*, *Lifted Brow*, *Voiceworks* and *Going Down Swinging*. She won the 2019 Fitzpatrick Award for creative nonfiction and was a finalist in the 2019 Swinburne Microfiction Competition. In 2020 she won the Mary River Press Short Story Prize. She's currently an MFA candidate at the University of Nevada, Las Vegas.

Jamieson Wolf has been writing since a young age when he realized he could be writing instead of paying attention in school. Since then, he has created many worlds in which to live his fantasies and live out his dreams.

He is a number-one bestselling author—he likes to tell people that a lot—and writes in many different genres. Jamieson is also an accomplished artist working with acrylic paint. He is also something of an amateur photographer and poet. He is also a Tarot reader.

He currently lives in Ottawa Ontario Canada with his husband Michael and their cat, Anakin who they swear has Jedi powers. You can visit Jamieson at www.jamiesonwolf.com

Matthew Del Papa graduated Laurentian University with a degree in English Literature in 1998. He joined the Sudbury Writers' Guild in 2009 and has since written for local newspapers and websites. His first book, *Jerry Lewis Told Me I Was Going to Die*—a collection of humorous essays about living with SMA— was released in 2023 from Latitude 46 Publishing. Currently at work on a novel, Matthew lives in Capreol, Ontario.

Holly Schofield travels through time at the rate of one second per second, oscillating between the alternate realities of city and country life. With over 100 published short stories, her works are used in university curricula and have been translated into multiple languages. Holly's stories have appeared in *Analog*, *Lightspeed*, *Escape Pod*, the Aurora-winning *Second Contacts*, and many other publications throughout the world. She hopes to save the world through science fiction and homegrown heritage tomatoes. Find her at hollyschofield. wordpress.com.

Erin Rockfort is an Ottawa-based writer, podcaster, and therapist. Her work has been featured in *Translunar Travelers Lounge*, *Ephemera Reading Series*, and *Nothing Without Us Too*. She also co-hosts the podcast *The Brodacious Book Club* and runs a book review blog on her website.

ACKNOWLEDGEMENTS

The editors would like to extend our gratitude to Nathan Frechette and everyone at Renaissance for embracing the vision of this book and helping bring it to life.

Thank you to the Canada Council for the Arts, for providing the funding to make this book possible.

To all of the disabled writers, storytellers and artists who are in these pages and beyond: your stories, resistance, and dreams matter, please keep sharing them with the world.

We would also like to thank the disabled community, especially Disabled Twitter, for the support, friendship, and camaraderie you've shown us. It is not always easy living and thriving in a world that wasn't designed with your accessibility in mind, but it's always appreciated to know that you aren't navigating it alone.

In creating this book, we sometimes struggled not to fall into the same familiar but harmful narratives and ideas Mighty is supposed to be fighting. We greatly value those who noticed our mistakes and helped us rectify them.

And finally, thank you for reading.

—Jennifer Lee Rossman and Emily Gillespie

Printed in the USA
CPSIA information can be obtained
at www.ICGtesting.com
CBHW051240211123
2010CB00042B/206